THE TRUTH OF DEATH

The Truth of Death

A SONJA AND CLAW MYSTERY

R. F. DeAngelis

M'Diro United

Contents

Dedication ix

Forward 1

Chapter 1
A Bad Night 4

Chapter 2
Mom 10

Chapter 3
.... 17

Chapter 4
.... 22

Chapter 5
Bar Hopping 29

Chapter 6
.... 34

Chapter 7
What's Your Emergency 40

Chapter 8   47

Chapter 9
Vengeance   52

Chapter 10   58

Chapter 11
Home is Where the Hurt Is   64

Chapter 12   70

Chapter 13
Favors & Bargains   76

Chapter 14   83

Chapter 15   90

Chapter 16
Big Red Button   96

Chapter 17
Donuts & Bad Dogs   102

Chapter 18
Siege Them   109

Chapter 19   115

Chapter 20
Sweet Kisses   121

Chapter 21
                                                126

Chapter 22
Grady   132

Chapter 23
                                                134

Chapter 24
                                                140

Chapter 25
A Trip to the Keys   145

Chapter 26
                                                152

Chapter 27
Pay the Ferryman   159

Chapter 28
                                                163

Chapter 29
Darker and Dumber   168

Chapter 30
                                                176

Chapter 31
Oh SH*T   181

Chapter 32
                                                                187
Chapter 33
                                                                194
Chapter 34
                                                                201
Epilogue
Back Home   207

About The Author   210
We're On The Web   211

As always thank you to my partners, my editor, and my beta readers. One of whom is the reason this novel exists.

Thank you Maria

A special thank you to my Patron Lynn

As always I dedicate this book to my daughter Raven

In Loving Memory of my little Brother
I miss you Berry

Copyright © 2024 by R. F. DeAngelis

All rights reserved. No part of this book may be reproduced in any manner whatsoever without written permission except in the case of brief quotations embodied in critical articles and reviews.

First Printing, 2024

Forward

Ok, look I've written the same things like six times and nothing I have written can prepare you for the weirdness that is about to follow. So, I'll start by introducing myself.

Hello *waves* my name is C.L.A.W.

When someone asks me what my name means, I tell them it's Cats Love All-out War. Kinda catchy, I think. But that's what it means to me. It is not what it meant written on the side of my cage, the wall of the facility I was made in, or the special bullshit acronym the military loves to name shit with. No, that's Cloned Living Animal Weapon.

Don't get me wrong. I was 'in' the military for certain values of the word in. I was engineered, trained, and the only survivor of a batch of 24 critters just like myself. Twelve male, twelve female. I think you can guess where that was going. I am a little over five foot ten, almost six foot if I go all the way up on my tip toes. I have orange and black hair, and a face meant for national geographic. I can and do walk on my hind legs and have thumbs, but running is far easier on all fours. My reflexes are, surprise, surprise, cat like, as is my eyesight and my hearing. The two radar dishes I got on top of my skull allow me to view sound three dimensionally, big bonus for what I was made for. If you haven't guessed by now, I am basically a Tiger Human hybrid. Granted some other things were thrown in. Some of it from the tiger in your house right now, the common house cat. If you're talking reaction time, you can't beat a cat.

Yes, I am a cat girl. No, I'm not a cute one. I only got enough human in me to let me think and speak, and have thumbs, and tits, why I have human tits is beyond me... but I digress. I spent the first part of my life being trained in a line of work that can best be described as both black and wet. I then spent a number of years in the cat box during the forever war. Kitty litter everywhere. It was a shitty experience.

No, there was no end date for my term of service, and my MOD doesn't exactly lend itself very well to civilian life, so the brass who actually knew I existed, well they figured I would leave feet first.

I had other ideas. Ideas that put a bounty on my head and led to me not only finding my best friend in the whole wide world, but to her making sure my asshole Uncle wouldn't come looking for me.

Weird enough yet?

Too bad, I'm the normal one.

No, I'm not kidding. A humanoid, force mutated tiger is the normal one in the story.

Everything is relative.

So, why am I writing this? A few reasons.

One I do not have a job. Not as such anyway. I do some odds and ends kind of stuff. No nothing black and nothing wet. More like "Oh can you possibly help me find this" kind of stuff. I also perform at conventions.

Two, when I tell the stories of what Sonja and I get up to, I get lots of people who are interested, and well, someone asked if I could write one of our adventures.

I got no idea if I can, mind you. I don't know if what I see her do, I can do justice to. But the third reason is why I'm doing this. Someone needs to know; someone needs to take up for this girl. Because, well, she's got other things to worry about.

So, buckle up and hope I find an amazing editor who can keep me on track.

Aside from the future. I found the best editor in the world. Oh god this was fun. I am so going to write another one.

Aside from the editor: I doubt I am the best editor in the world, but I loved working on this book and hopefully made it as easy to read as possible. >^.^<

Chapter 1

A Bad Night

Today was not a normal day. A normal day would see her working out with one of her wooden wasters. Short sword and up, she has one and practices. I've been trained in martial combat, both armed and unarmed, as well as a variety of toys. Her? She knows the guards, she knows the strikes, she's been taught... something. What I'm not sure, but something. Mornings for her normally start about 10:30, 11... 12... when I get there. Sometimes she doesn't wake up then.

Bedtime is whenever she falls asleep.

So, as you probably guess, when I came at 6 am to find her sitting on her couch, staring at the TV and a news report about the Synagogue fire, I knew something was up.

God, how to describe Sonja? Ok she's five eight, 170 lbs., with red hair that had black, blond, brown, and white in it. It all depends on what the light is doing to her at the moment. Same with her eyes. They're grey, except for when they are Disney villain green, or steel blue… or, well you get the idea. She is muscular, but it's the old school Celtic or Norse muscle. She's goth, so most of her clothing is some shade of black that she swears she can tell the difference between.

None of that does her justice. If I may get poetic for a moment, she has eyes that flash like blades, quick, precise. She has a lopsided smile that can light up a whole room, and she knows how to use it. When she's happy the room warms. When she's upset the room gets colder. Wait. That's not actually poetic, that part is literal.

sighs What she is, is fun, warm, thoughtful, empathetic, nice, hard, cold, distant, frightening, all rolled into one depending on her mood. Is she good looking? I don't know, she's human, I'm a cat. I know some humans really seem to dig her.

Sonja and her roommate Mortis live in an old warehouse that a friend of ours bought just for her. She has a bed, a couch, a tv, a shower, a tub, a stove, and a fridge. Also, a horse trough and hay, but that's for Mortis.

Her roommate is a horse. He's not her pet, he's her partner. He is also intelligent. Like me and you, intelligent. Kyle's horse Midnight is smart and self-aware, but he thinks like a horse.

Mortis doesn't.

Midnight will talk to anyone, usually to freak them out since he does it telepathically.

Mortis talks when he wants to, not before. It's also not telepathic. Don't get me wrong, he's not mister Ed. His lips don't move. But you know what he said. You heard him. Even if you are telepathically a null, if that damn horse wants you to know what he thinks, you will know.

Oh, it gets worse.

He's ash gray. He's also built like a shire.

She treats him like any 16-year-old treats her horse. Oh yes, when it comes to him, she's a total horse girl. Granted, that's about the only normal thing she does. She's also not 16. Not by a long shot. I think she's in her late 30s... I think. Oh, she looked to be in her 20s. But seeing as I have known her for fifteen years, she most certainly is not.

So, no, seeing her curled up on her couch, crying, watching the morning news was not how I expected to start my day.

I was going to make her breakfast.

Look, I love the girl, she's one of the smartest people I know. But when it comes to taking care of herself, she forgets. A lot. Kyle says its C-PTSD, ADHD, Autism, and Dissociative Disorder. To me, she's just her.

"Hey toots, you're up early."

A sort of wave was my only answer. On my way to the area she had made into her kitchen, I walked by the horse. "How bad?"

<**Up until a little after two, back up at five. She's been staring at that screen since then.**>

Oh boy.

I went over and made her a southern breakfast. Grits, eggs, bacon, sausage, toast, and coffee. Once it was done, I then mixed it all together, well all but the toast and coffee, and threw some cheese in. She was a comfort eater, and well this was something her mom made for her. I put the heavily buttered toast, which was cut diagonally, in point first. Her coffee was sweet and light.

I had seen her drink it black. In fact, I had seen her drink it every way possible except black with sugar. That she didn't like.

Taking it all over to her, I sat beside her and put the bowl in her lap. "Want to talk about it?"

She kept staring at the TV. "I'm just tired."

"Bad night?"

"Nightmare."

"About?" What she called nightmares and what I called nightmares were vastly different things.

She shrugged. "I got up, walked outside, saw the sky as blood red. Started trying to talk to people, ask what's going on, warn people, whatever. It didn't matter. No matter how much I yelled, my voice was so quiet no one heard me."

Trust me, it wasn't the bloody sky that messed her up. "Want to go out today?"

Her head tilted to the side. "Maybe after."

Uh-oh. "After what?" The words weren't out of my mouth when I heard the sound of a text hit my ears. "Shit."

She shrugged. "It's not that bad." She blinked, "Not yet."

I gave it a quick read. It was my 'work' phone. Like I said, I do odds and ends kind of stuff. Follow ex-wife, spy on former husband, a lot of lawyers hire me, a lot of divorce lawyers.

A girl's got to eat.

::You were recommended by a friend of mine, Charles Stanton. He said you were discrete and could help. I've tried the cops, they are not as helpful as I hoped. Please, can we at least meet?::

Well shit. Charles was a regular, usually had me doing a lot of leg work for him. I was good at the human side of this biz despite never receiving a day of training in it. People like to talk to me, and it lets me find a lot of people who didn't want to be found. Granted this was usually where cheating spouse x was shacking up with and who, but it still counted.

Whoever this was, they weren't a lawyer. Lawyers always start off with 'HI I'm A. Lawyer. I Work for Dewey, Cheatem, and Howl.' The police aren't as much help as I hoped wasn't a good sign either.

But she saw it coming.

::Sure, I would love to meet. I take it you have been told the particulars about myself?::

::Money isn't an issue, nor is the fact that you are different. I don't have a lot of interactions with you people, but Charles says you are the best, and that you're basically the only person he can think of at all with your track record.::

You People, wonderful. I looked over at Sonja. She was still watching TV but at least she was stuffing her face. This might get her out of her funk. Especially if it was something that the cops couldn't help with. What I love most about her is the fact that she seems incapable of turning down anyone in need, even if she's not a fan of them.

I gave Miss... Mr? You People, the address, told them to bring coffee, and that if my partner was good with the case, we would help out.

After that? Well, Sonja wasn't in pajamas. I don't think she owns any.

"Oh kay, up. We got company, and possibly a job.

Mechanically, she stopped chewing, swallowed and got up and went over to her clothing rack to get dressed.

Oh boy, this wasn't good.

I watched as she moved robotically, took a quick shower, got out, dried off, pulled her clothing on as if she were doing it from instructions she got off the internet and this was her third time, then sit down and do her make up. That she actually took some care with. There are times when I act more human than she does. It's like she's not quite tethered to her meat suit. As she went around getting ready, she downed another cup of coffee, then went over to the mirror and 'masked up'. Zero to human in no time flat. I had watched her do that for years, and to be honest? It kind of broke my heart for her.

Chapter 2

Mom

It didn't take long before my phone chimed once more.
::I'm here, are you sure this is the correct address?::
Good question. I mean I gave her the right address, that didn't mean she was at the right place. I hopped up and went to the door and stuck my head out.

The alley outside was a New York Alley, cleaner than some, dirtier than most. Nothing stank, ok so that had more to do with the time of year than the cleanliness of the alley. New York is not the cesspool TV tries to make it out to be. People are people and here people are everywhere. The main good thing about it is the fact that the morning sun didn't hit it. That meant it didn't come in the windows, not that that matters as she's covered them all with automatic shutters.

Yes, she was at the right place. Middle aged, European diaspora, most likely English, probably didn't think of herself as white so much as 'normal' but would probably fight you on her being proud to be white. Brown eyes, brownish blonde hair with more than a hint of silver streaked through. The clothing wasn't just modest, it was almost puritanical, long flowing skirt, arms fully covered, her powder blue blouse buttoned all the way to her throat. As soon as she saw me, a fear response hit her and she backed up half a step, fear mingling with her mild floral perfume.

Thinking quickly, I blepped. I watched as her human brain short circuited. It didn't matter that I was a tiger, suddenly all that mattered was I was a cat. She smiled at me and her face relaxed.

"Claw?" She asked, her voice somewhere between awe how cute and I'm still not sure I'm in the right place.

I made my eyes as huge as I could. "Yes ma'am."

She blushed. "I wasn't expecting..." Her voice trailed off.

I nodded. "Yes ma'am, I'm southern. Born in Texas and spent most of my childhood is Georgia." All ten years of it. She didn't need to know that.

She actually shook her head and chuckled in relief. "He said you were a cat person, I just didn't think it was quite this literal." She got ahold of herself and tried again. "I'm sorry, my name is Abigail Smith. My friend, Mr. Stanton said you were not only willing to work for someone in need, but you were also good at finding things, and people."

Her accent was rural, but it was rural Massachusetts. Her eyes were quick, and her posture was proper. Her purse was plain, functional, and large enough it probably held everything a mother could need from day to day.

I pursed my lips. It was for effect, it let humans know I was thinking, but such a facial affectation wasn't natural for me. "Yes well, I can't promise anything until I've heard what the job is. Would you please come in?"

She smiled and took a step forward, then stopped in her tracks. "Hold on, the coffee is in the car. I didn't want to bring it out if I didn't have the right place." With that she turned and dashed off back to her car, her sensible car, in her sensible shoes, and she had brought several cups. "I didn't know how much or what kind to get. So, I got two blacks, two cappuccinos, and two lattés."

I stepped out and helped her bring all that in. "It's not actually for me, it's for my associate." With that we both went inside. She stopped almost immediately, and I took a second to realize what this place must look like to her.

Large open area, huge unmade bed, racks of clothing, all black, a black leather couch, chains hanging from the rafters, a collection of wooden swords arranged on one wall, a TV set up to be a monitor to a computer that already had 4 monitors in front of an old office chair. Off to the left it looked like a normal kitchen but one with one of those fancy stoves. But on the right was a horse, a huge horse, with a goth girl currently curry combing it.

Sonja turned as she heard us come back in, and despite the fact that she was doing her best to mask, she looked like a possessed porcelain doll. White skin, huge round eyes, and a smile.

Mrs. Smith nearly bolted.

"And this is Sonja. She's my, well, she see's things."

"Like a psychic?"

Sonja came forward, "No ma'am, more like a huckster that cold reads you at a carnival. I pick up clues and such most miss." As she did she offered her hand, her dagger point nails clawed hand.

But Mrs. Smith took it without seeming to notice. "Well, that's different. How did you two meet?"

The smile this time wasn't fake. "I was a starving artist and she stumbled into my studio." That's when the coffee hit her nose. "Coffee?" This time her eyes lit up for real and Mrs. Smith relaxed a little more.

"Why, yes. Ms. Claw said to bring it." At that Sonja did a little bow thing that looked like it came out of some period drama and took the coffee from her and made her way over to the counter. Once she set the six down, she turned the first one up.

Mrs. Smith leaned in and whispered, "She's autistic, isn't she?"

I blinked. "I see we're not the only ones who are paying attention."

She smiled. "My sister's boy is as well. She was stimming as she was walking over. Bad night I take it?"

I nodded, "Normally she wouldn't even be up yet for a few hours." I watched in horror as Sonja did as I knew she would, she turned up the newest dose of caffeine and started sucking it down as well. Breathing for her was occasionally optional. Her noticing made me think better of her, well her noticing and not assuming Sonja was somehow lesser. "So, what's the issue Charles thinks I can help you with?"

Just that quick, I watched as her eyes clouded over. "My son, he's dead. Someone shot him in the back. I want you to find out why, of course, but..." She swallowed hard, "I also want you to find out who he was." She took a tissue out of her purse and dabbled at her eyes. "My boy was always special, a real artist type. When he turned 18, he, he went away. Kind of a gone and never came back thing. He and his father didn't get along." She let out a defeated chuckle. "Heavens, the last night he was at home, we all had this huge fight. Said we didn't care about him, didn't notice him or see him for who he was, just who we wanted him to be. Accused us of caring more about our church than him."

Sonja's head whipped up at that. "Evangelical." It wasn't a question.

She nodded. "Yes." She sighed. "It became a point of contention between him and his father. Then he accused me of always taking his dad's side and never his because, because I was brainwashed and couldn't think for myself." She sort of smiled. "My husband, he's a hard man, but a fair one. He knows I'm here, but he doesn't think you can find anything and wished I would let it go."

"You said the cops couldn't help?" I asked. If the kid was dead, and the cops couldn't help, I doubted we could do anything.

She took a deep breath. "That's why Charles recommended you, he said you were good and you were discrete. My son was found dead yesterday. He'd been shot. They have no suspects, but... he was..." She choked up at that point. The tears were real, you can smell the difference between the different types. This was grief, and whatever it was, it was bad. "He was found wearing a dress and had a balloon full of drugs in his stomach that they found during the autopsy." She looked at me, pleading in her eyes. "My boy hated drugs. He was always shy, sensitive, not outgoing at all. He just wasn't the type. I, I'd like to find out who did this to him, but more, I want to find out what happened to my baby."

Sonja walked up. "What are the cops saying Mrs. Smith?"

"They are saying he was a mule, and that he was killed for it." She shook her head. "They're wrong."

Mrs. Smith blinked at Sonja. "How can you be sure?"

"The drugs were still in her stomach; the killer didn't know they were there. So, it can't be the person who was paying her to move them."

"Do, do you think my son got mixed up with the wrong crowd?"

She pursed her lips, her eyes cut over to me. "Um, I think that's a given. But..." Vice would have this, and it sounded like they already wrote it off. Meaning he wasn't a known mule. "We can't make any guarantees, but" That was as far as I got.

"But no matter what, you won't like what we find."

"How can you say that?" Her tone was defensive.

"Well, one, you have an idea of your child that is firmly in your mind, the chances we will find that child are less than zero. Right now, you're hurt, confused, and upset. But you still have that picture of your kid. We look into this, and you may find out what your child meant when they said you didn't see them. Kids, they ghost parents for a number of reasons. A lot of the time, it's to spare parents the pain of the truth."

Her chin went up. "If you are implying I was a bad mother," she sighed, "I've already come to that conclusion myself. I haven't seen my child in five years, and... I knew nothing of them. It's too late for me to get to know my kid, but I can at least remember them for who they really were... no matter how painful that might be."

Sonja walked up. "My word, we will find what you seek."

Well shit. I mean I was going to say yes, but this went beyond yes. The woman didn't know it yet, but she just got told that she would be told the whole unvarnished truth.

Like it.

Lump it.

Live with it.

Chapter 3

Mrs. Smith handed us the few personal effects that the police had found on her son at the time of his death. It consisted of a match book (who still used those?), a purse full of condoms, a gray plastic electronic id card with no writing on it, and a bloody dress.

"I have a picture of him, from high school. It was the last one we had." As Sonja was looking over the effects, I took the picture from her. Hair was short, eyes were bright, but there wasn't any joy in them despite the smile on the kid's face.

"The cops said that was what he was wearing when they found him. There was no wallet, no ID, credit card or anything." She swallowed hard. "Given the outfit… I'm terrified he was doing 'things' for money." She said things as if it was the dirtiest concept she could imagine. So dirty in fact that she couldn't put words to it.

Sonja had taken the things out of the plastic bag they were in. "They weren't a prostitute if that's what you're worried about?"

She blinked. "How, how can you be sure?"

Sonja took a breath. "The purse is too high end. Out of style mind you, but it's an older Chanel. She could have sold it for" Sonja looked it over, "About two grand easy. As such, she would most likely have done so if she were needing to turn tricks to live."

Mrs. Smith blinked, "That, makes no sense. If... did you say she?"

Sonja nodded. "The makeup stains here aren't drag level" she was plundering in the purse, "it's a little pricey mind you." She smelled the purse. "I'd say Mac." She nodded to herself, "Good stuff but not for the stage, usually. So, she wasn't drag or a stripper." She took out one of the condoms from the plastic bag. "And these are all Trigen. Not the cheapest nor most expensive. In other words, she bought them instead of getting them from a clinic or shelter."

"Why do you keep saying she?"

Sonja looked her in the eye. "Because this is," she gestured at the dress, the purse, etc, "The trappings of a woman, not a professional, not an entertainer." She seemed to think about it for a moment. "She had a job, and one that she needed to look a certain way for," she took out the gray card. "A place with good security for the employees, but not something the patrons had to worry about."

"I'm sorry, but are you saying my son was a freak?"

Sonja's face darkened. "No, I'm saying your daughter was a lower middle class 20 something living in New York. I'm surprised that I've managed to upset you already. You said you wanted to know."

The woman shook her head, tears started to well up in her eyes. "I'm, I'm just trying to get my head around it. My little boy, was living as a woman and running drugs... it's, a lot."

I looked at the woman with pity. "Look, I'm sorry. This must be hard to hear but..."

"I mean how could you know all of this from just the purse?"

Sonja sighed. "First off as I said, if she had been hard up for money, she could have just sold the purse. Second, it's out of date and well used. It was probably a gift. Maybe even from an admirer. As for the drugs, that wasn't her modus operandi. Your daughter wasn't a junky."

Mrs. Smith put her hand up to her mouth, then spoke. "Now you're just trying to make me feel better." She wiped the tears from her face.

"Actually, I don't think she is. She has a point. If your child was so hard up for money that they turned to this, why not pawn the purse way before it got that bad?"

Sonja, whether oblivious to the woman needing more time, or not caring, added. "I don't think this was a mugging either. While the wallet was gone, the purse was left. Even if the thieves didn't know what it was, they should have taken it and tried to pawn it. The fact that they didn't, the level of brutality, and the theft that wasn't a theft, means someone didn't want her to be found and connected to who she was. They tried to erase her." Sonja cocked her head. "How did the police identify her anyway?"

"His school. They were still doing the fingerprint your child thing when he was in fifth grade. We got a card with his prints and full name on it, 'Samual Aaron Smith' and his cute little picture." She handed that over too. This picture of the kid actually looked happier than the older one. "It didn't occur to me or his father at the time that that could be used to track us. God, that sounds so silly now." She was crying openly, but no longer seemed to care. "By the time my youngest was old enough we declined it, but I guess in this case it was a good thing." She straightened up. "So, you're telling me my son was my daughter, wasn't a, a prostitute, and that she wasn't a drug user?" Sonja nodded. "Well then. You've already told me more than the police."

Sonja pursed her lips. "We can stop here if you want, as I said, you won't like what we find."

Abigail Smith steeled herself. "I don't care. Find out who my child was... who he, she was, and if you can, who did this to her and why."

Sonja nodded. "Claw and I will be in touch."

I got up. "May I walk you to your car?" When the woman nodded, I got up and led her outside. "I'm sorry my colleague is a little blunt."

"She's alright. I know that autism makes empathy hard for them."

I stopped, "Actually the opposite. She's very empathetic, she just doesn't understand why you humans lie to each other and yourselves."

The woman nodded. "I guess we do, don't we." Her chin went up. "I always told myself I was doing a good job with my children. Now, my youngest still lives at home but grows more distant every day, and my oldest... my oldest is dead and all because I couldn't, didn't..." At that she broke down crying.

I pulled her in and hugged her. It was the only thing I could think to do. Well, not the only thing. I did have house cat in me. I started purring as I petted her head and comforted her.

It took a while, but she calmed, then pulled back, "Are you, are you purring?"

I nodded. "Most of me is Panthera, some is feline."

She shook her head. "I'll never quite understand you powered. I really won't."

I shrugged. "That's ok. I don't understand me either. It's why I gotz a translation thingy. Smart ass to common sense."

She laughed. "Please, keep me informed. I, I know this isn't going to be easy for me. But, I need, not want, I need to face this."

I so wanted to say 'you got it toots' to her at that. In my head it was funny. I also knew the human wouldn't appreciate it. So, I did something I've been practicing for years, but am not very good at. Shutting up.

I nodded to her.

She nodded to me, then crawled back into her suburban soccer mom mobile and drove off. I turned around and went back inside. Sonja would already be working, and I needed to keep up.

Chapter 4

"She gone?" Sonja was already sitting at her desk, typing away at her computer.

"Yep. So, what didn't you tell her?" Shutting the door, I made my way over to her.

"That the purse smelled of beer."

"So, she was a drinker?"

"Possible, but if she was this will be a dead end."

I looked at the screen she was using. "You know New York doesn't require a bartender to have a liquor license, right?" She stopped her typing. "What makes you think she was a bartender?"

She sighed and leaned back. "A hunch. I mean, the purse is basically saturated in the smell. Which means either she spilled something on it, or it was around it long enough to soak into the fabric."

"Maybe that's why she didn't sell it." She gave me a look at that. "What? It's possible."

"Claw, this is New York. She could stand off 5th and hock it for a couple hundred bucks if she wanted to, and it would be no questions asked."

I sat down "Well that's stupid." Stretching I yawned. "I mean, it's just a purse."

"It's a Chanel, trust me, fake ones go for a few hundred dollars on street corners." She sighed in defeat. "Well, if she doesn't have to be licensed, I am open to suggestions of how we find out where a trans bartender worked."

Rolling my eyes, I pushed her over to the side and typed on her keyboard.

"Bar Crawl dot com?"

I shrugged. "It's going to have a lot of pictures of boozers and bartenders sometimes get caught in the photos."

"Oh and?"

"And... geo tags?" I watched her face palm. "Forgot that was a thing?"

"It slipped my mind."

I chuckled, "Well as slippery as your mind is, you should have been first in line."

She grinned at me. "Oh, I was first in line, until the little hair ball was born."

I loved quoting movies, and she never let me down. Well, almost never. It also cheered her up. "I'm going to go make a few phone calls, see if I can shake some info loose. You see if you can spot our girl in the background."

She nodded and clicked on pictures. As she started clicking her mouse, she started out slow. As she went on, she got faster and faster. I knew she was scanning the photos, but to be honest I still didn't know how she did it that fast.

Taking out my phone, I called a cop friend of ours.

The phone connection clicked on the second ring, "Savage."

"Yes, I would like a large bacon cheese burger, extra fries, and a shake."

"I'll shake you, cat. What do you need?"

"Need anything you can get me on a mule that died a few nights ago. The name is Samuel Aaron Smith." I picked up pen and paper.

"Hold on."

I could hear him typing away. Honestly it wouldn't have been bad, but typing has its own unique accent. As far as I could tell, no two people typed in the same rhythm. In one ear was Kyle's methodical click clack of his mechanical keyboard. In my other, when Sonja wasn't speed clicking her mouse as if she were trying to match the rate of fire of an automatic to the rat tat tat of a machine gun, she was hunting and pecking away at her keys. To be fair, she typed with two fingers better than I did with my hands on home row.

"Got 'em. Male, a single GSW. Also severe bruising and cracked ribs. She took a hell of a beating. Looks like they were going with a hate crime until the autopsy."

"Yeah, they found drugs, but Sonja is still betting on hate crime. If they knew about drugs, why no take drugs?"

"It's possible, but this has already been buried in the pile." He signed. "Too low priority. I'm taking it Simple and Simon are on the case."

"Ha ha… wait, which of us is simple?"

"Of the two of you? Think about it fuzzy."

"Ow, that hurt. At least I can grow a beard."

"You are a beard."

"True."

"Seriously, are you two on this?"

"Yeah, mom just stopped by, wants us to find out what happened to her kid."

"Good luck. I'll send you what I'm allowed to."

"Please and thank you."

"You got it." With that he hung up. I walked back over to the mad clicker. "Any luck?"

She gave me a shrug. "While not a bad idea, these people aren't taking pictures of bartenders, so I'm looking for hair color and style." Each photo flashed up on the screen for less than a second before she was on to the next one. In fact, she went through about three per second. So about 180 a minute.

"How do you know what her hair looks like?"

"Crime scene photos." Finally, she stopped and sat back. "Bingo. Short cropped, black hair, pale skin, brown eyes, and about five and half feet given those shelves."

I took a look. There on screen was two party girls having the time of their lives going by the way they were throwing up peace signs and duck faces. Behind them was a punk, a real one, she was mixing in a shaker. "It's a place to start. Where is this?"

Sonja pointed at the neon sign behind the bar. It was a blue circle, seven red number eights were equally spaced round it. Seven eights was a mid-end bar and night spot, their normal clientele ran the gambit, but mostly consisted of girls like the ones in the picture and the boys that hit on them. That was after six thirty of course. It's daytime crowd ran more to the 'let's get out of the office and grab some lunch and a drink' crowd. It was trendy enough to take a client to, to impress them, but still low key enough for suits to get in.

Sonja smiled at me. "It's a start."

We walked outside, and I realized I wasn't going to need my bike. In front of the door was a beautiful grey, pearlescent '69 sting ray. As Sonja walked around to the driver's side, the door opened for her before she got to it. I had to open my own door.

As we both sat down, and Sonja put her hands on the wheel, the car roared to life. It was an angry sound, a predatory sound. Sonja looked at the console then petted the dash.

"I know, I know. She was a bitch. But she's trying." The last part was hopeful. "And we got some good leads. So could you please take us to Seven Eights?"

The car's engine sounded less angry somehow as it put itself in gear and began driving itself. Sonja kept her hands on the wheel so things didn't look out of place, but it was the car calling the shots. Something made evident when it took us to Pop's Store rather than where we asked.

"Um, why are we here?"

Sonja pursed her lips and looked out of the window, then sighed. "Pop's has fresh apples in."

With a resigned looked she got out and went inside.

That left me with a rare opportunity, it left me and 'The Transportation' alone.

"So, um. Like, I've seen you horse, and I've seen you bike. Why a car?"

<**She likes this car, and I am trying to get her in a better mood. Maybe she'll sleep.**>

That made sense. Mortis and I didn't always see eye to eye, but I knew he was as devoted to her as I was. Come to think of it, she was the only thing we really agreed on.

"So, you can be anything?"

< I am the transportation; I am what she needs me to be.>

I knew Mortis was some kind of magic creature, and that he'd been named after death's horse. To be honest, had it been me, I would have named him Binky. "So, whatever she needs?"

<whatever transportation she needs>

"Ok, so why do you usually look like a horse?"

<She like's horses, has since she was a little girl>

That made sense, come to think of it, it explained the beast's coloration as well. Sonja was, first and foremost, a Christian, and second, she was goth. She had her own pale horse and named him Mortis. Granted, I had no idea what kind of 'Christian' she was, but she definitely tried to live up to him, or her interpretation of him anyway. She didn't care about the LGBTQIA+ crowd, well she did, but not like other Christians I had met. She believed in helping them. She believes in helping anyone. So much so, I thought she was better off just dropping the 'Christian' title. After all, she didn't act anything like them as far as I could tell.

"So, what do you really look like?"

<I am the transportation>

"You realize that doesn't narrow it down, right?" Did you ever feel like a car just shrugged at you? Because I did, I did right now.

The driver's side door popped open and the seat went forward. Sonja slid a couple of bags of apples into the space then hopped back in.

"Ok horse face, you want them, you got to behave. Deal?"

<define behave>

She let out a sigh, "Don't do anything Midnight would consider fun. I swear that horse is a bad influence on you."

<he said I don't horse well, and he was teaching me how to be a more believable horse>

Well, I certainly couldn't argue with that. Other than eat and poop out charcoal briquettes, Mortis didn't act much like a horse.

Sonja, however, could argue. "Midnight is a short-eared jackass. And that's according to Kyle. If you're trying to be more horse like, why not try acting like Lady?"

<she's a girl horse, I'm supposed to be a boy horse>

She left out a defeated sigh. "We have to get you some male friends. Now take us to the damn bar."

<Okiedokie>

With that the car started back up and drove to Seven Eights.

Chapter 5

Bar Hopping

We got to the place well before nine, and that was the problem, it wasn't open yet. What was more, we were parked in a no parking zone. I looked around and wondered how long it would take for us to be yelled at, ticketed, booted, and of course towed. Could Mortis be towed?

"Um, hun?"

Sonja looked over at me, "Yes?"

I pointed, first at the building, then at the sign. "What are we doing?" I hadn't meant for it to, but the question came out sing song.

She looked at me as if I had lost reason. "We're waiting. We want to catch them when they are not busy with people, and waiting 'til we see someone pull into that parking lot right over there." She pointed and I could see a private parking area just off to the side of the building. "And we're parked here so we can watch that lot," she adjusted the mirror, "and the front door. As for the no parking? No one will bother us."

I pursed my little lips. "How can you be so sure, are we invisible?"

She rolled her eyes. "Hardly. One, that takes a lot of energy and concentration, two, people tend to notice invisible things."

"Um, no. I mean, that's what invisible is, they can't see us."

She nodded. "Exactly. They can't see something invisible. So anything, like say a leaf, or a runaway newspaper, or flier or any kind of trash, stops on the spot where nothing is, and stays there. Then that looks out of place and draws attention."

Ok, that made sense. Mortis didn't usually do car. Normally he does a bike and her and I can park in the alley. This was the first time I had been in the horse when it was a car.

"So, we're not invisible, that means as soon as some meter maid or traffic cop sees us, you're going to be ticketed."

"Nope, we're something better than invisible."

I had to know. "I'll bite."

"We're someone else's problem."

I looked at her incredulously, "How does that work?"

She cocked her head. "Well, I got the name for it from a book." Of course she did. "But like, it was happening anyway. It's just the best way I have of describing it."

"Well, for those of us that aren't as well read as you?"

"Oh, yeah. Well. We're parked illegally, someone sees us. It's not their problem, they don't have to worry about us, someone else will take care of it. If normally they would call the cops, they would assume someone already has. If a cop comes by, they will think that we're just here for a moment, then we'll move on, so it's not worth the time to bust us. No one else will try to park here because, well, someone has already parked here."

I blinked. "And that works?"

She pursed her lips. "Close your eyes."

I did. "Ok, now what?"

Her voice grew sad. "How many homeless people are there on this block?"

"How..." I thought about it. I was a predator, a hunter, I worked for Uncle Sam and was trained to always observe.

I couldn't remember seeing a homeless person.

"Exactly. Someone else's problem. We've all been trained to ignore it if there's nothing we can do about it."

I opened my eyes and looked around. Woman by the dumpster, man on the corner, a couple walking hand in hand in the ally.

"Fuck."

"Yep."

"So, we're someone else's problem?"

"Yes, we are."

"What if, what if someone sees us and decides we are their problem?"

"Then they needed to see us." She shrugged. "It's not perfect."

We sat there as time ticked on, we were in a stake out, sort of. The angle of the light changed, the shadows grew shorter, and the traffic picked up a bit. I was watching the bar, and so was Sonja.

Which meant both of us jumped out of our skin when there was a knock on the window. So much for someone else's problem.

I turned to look at she who had penetrated their apathy so that they might gaze upon our splendor, and froze mid breath.

Samuel Smith, or whatever she'd named herself, was standing right outside the window looking at the two of us as if we had personally annoyed or offended her in some way. Nice spiked short black hair, good make up job, a few pieces of face jewelry that were both understated in size and color, and still ostentatious in their number. She was also very much alive.

Hanging around Sonja, I had seen ghosts. This wasn't one.

Sonja cranked down the window. "Yes?"

"What the hell are you wankers doing here. This is a no parking zone i'n't it? Plus, you two been ogling the front for the entire time you been here." She then took her eyes off Sonja and looked at me, "And you kitty cat, ya peepin me like ya seen a ghost."

Sonja gave a sad smile. "She has, do you mind if we ask you a few questions?"

She went from outrage to skeptical, "You two cops? Immigration? I swear my paperwork is up to date."

I smiled at her, "No nothing like that, just wanting to know if you know a Samuel Smith."

She nodded. "Ya back in the east end. Why? What he got to do with anything? He come state side too? Looking for a good word, cuz I ain't got one for him."

Sonja shook her head. "Do you recognize this person?" She held out the photo she had printed off from Bar Crawl.

Our east end friend took a look and her eyes narrowed. "What you want with Rayray?"

I frowned. "Ray?" I looked at Sonja. Unusual for her to be that off.

"Yeah, Rayzor. You two looking to give her a hard time or something? You ain't with that wanker are you?"

Sonja stopped her. "I don't believe we're with anyone, and we're trying to find out what happened to her."

"Wa'da'ya'mean what happened to her?"

I looked at her. "She's dead, we're trying to find out why."

All of the color drained out of her already pale face, her breathing went rapid, her legs started to buckle, then her eyes rolled into the back of her head. "She's dead?" She managed to breath out as her ass hit the ground.

Chapter 6

Inside the bar, things were dark and only the bare minimum light needed to do the stocking was available. Sonja and I had both managed to help the young lady to the door, and a guy who had more in common with a brick wall than most other men took one look at his friend not doing well and had helped us get her inside.

"She can't be dead. She's off with that creeper who keeps sniffing her crotch." She looked up from the floor to Sonja then to me. "I mean he just took her to Mexico for her vacation."

"She was found three days ago, right here in New York."

Tears started to make tracks on her makeup. "That can't be right, they ain't the cops came here looking for her?"

I went to explain, but Sonja cut me off. "Her mother hired us. She wants to find out what happened, and, well, the cops don't see it as a priority."

"Bloody hell." With those words she went off into a tirade about how fucking useless the cops were. At least, that's what I think she said. To be honest she was talking way to fast and saying words that sounded like English, but didn't translate. Something about the lot of them being Berks, something vehement about cobblers' and how best to kick them with daisies, and something about stupid ducks and geese and how if she did to them what she wanted she'd end up in the 'Flowery Dell'. She then said she wished she had an oily rag.

At that point Sonja pulled out a cigarette and handed it to her. I blinked. "You understood that?"

She shrugged, "I grew up watching the PBS and they had a lot of British shows, especially sci-fi and dramas." She looked at the girl. "How long have you been state side?"

"Couple of years. Since some slag made me asbo and I wasn't living with that. Came to the rotten apple cuz you septics dig anything that sounds bri'ish."

"How did you know Rayray?"

She looked at me like I was stupid, "It's New York in'it? How do you think I knew her? We was roommates. Duke of Kent here is stupid." She sighed. "Brass tacks, you on the up and up?" She took a deep breath and calmed herself. "Sorry, know you don't follow. Are you bein' honest with me?"

"Yes." Sonja and I said at the same time.

"Then you got to know, her and her mum, they didn't see eye to eye right? Used to tear her up cuz she loved her mum. But something happened, something big. Rayzor never talk about it to me."

"Why do you two look so much alike?"

"Well, we both were looking for a place when we bumped into each other on a message board. She had her picture, I had mine. Except for the eye color we could be twins. Well that, and that mom of hers never showed her makeup. Don't get me wrong, it wasn't bad, but it wasn't good."

Sonja decided this was the perfect time to drop a bomb. "She didn't show her daughter how to do makeup because she thought her daughter was her son."

The girl looked at us. "Rayzor? Trans? No mate." Sonja held up the picture again, and she took it out of her hand and stared out it. "Heavens, why didn't she tell me."

"Possibly she didn't think you would take it well." I said.

A man came out of the back. "Blade! You need to clock in, I got shit for you to do."

"Fuck off Rob, Rayzor's dead."

Rob stopped dead in his tracks. "What?"

Blade, as we now had a name for her, pointed at the two of us. "Couple of private dicks her mum hired to find out what happened."

Rob turned pale. "Fuck." He looked over at her. "You ok? I know, I mean, you're, I mean. I know you two were close. You ok?"

"No you bleeding wanker, I'm not ok." She snapped.

Rob held up both hands in surrender. "Look, you need to go home?"

Blade wiped her face. "Yes, no, I don't know." She took a deep breath. "I need to think. She wasn't even s'pose to be home til the weekend." She got a far off look on her face, one I sadly knew. The look of someone who had known pain one time too many. "Place is trashed. Was gonna clean up tomorrow."

Rob put a hand on her shoulder. "Look, go home." He then turned to us, "You two. Come back after close." He shook his head, "I'm going to go over some of the takes, see if I see anything odd. I'll gladly answer any questions you have." He nodded to himself, then walked off.

"We was twins you know. That's what we told people. She helped me with the American slang and shit and how to be better understood by these bunch of yanks. I get thick sometimes. I taught her how to sound like a proper Londoner. She loved everyone thinking we was sisters. Guess…" She shook her head. "Damn, guess that explains why she never hit on me."

I nodded. "You mind if we go to your place. It might help us find out what happened."

"Sure mate…sure." With that she was back to the thousand-yard stare.

I looked over at Sonja and made a motion with my head to give the girl some time. She nodded, and both of us moved off to give her some space.

"Talk to me space cadet." I said in a low voice.

"She's hurt, it's not the first time. She honestly didn't know, but she knows something even if she doesn't know what yet. Rob is a bit clueless, but seems ok. He has known something's up for a while. He was shocked when he was first told, but his mind started seizing on something right after." She nodded to herself and looked at Blade again. "They're punk, hell she's a British punk. But the names? The look?"

"Think they got a little bat cave in them?"

"Maybe. Prot goth maybe?" She shook her head. "I'll know more once I see her not at work."

"Fair. Digested the mom yet?"

She nodded. "Evangelical, blames herself. She's chafing under something and is looking for an excuse to lash out. Her dead kid's going to give her one. She been suppressing unhappy for a while, goes back to before the kid even fucked off." She nodded. "The wound on her heart is raw, bleeding, but it's not new. This has been building for a while."

When it came to insight, Sonja was remarkably perceptive... as long as it wasn't social cues. As she put it, she didn't see the lies, only the truth, the pain.

"So, grab the girl, head to her place?"

Sonja's head snapped around, and her eyes locked with a guy that had just pushed his way into the interior from off the street. He was whip thin and jittery, and only had eyes for Blade. At least until he scoped us out as he looked around. He saw me, and his eyes grew narrow, he saw Sonja, and he bolted.

Running from predators is a good way to get chased.

Think about that when it comes to cops...

I managed to make it all the way to the door before I had to hit all fours. Sonja didn't have that problem. I'm scary. I mean, other than the clothing I was wearing, I was now a couple hundred pounds of tiger chasing a man down the street. Sonja, first off was somehow faster than I was, and second, the guy was way more scared of her than me. Third, Sonja was leaning forward, not so much running as falling and catching herself with her next step as she did so.

The longer this went on, the faster she got.

Mister unlucky made a dive for an alleyway and threw a big green plastic garbage thing, the one on wheels for regular trash that's not actually a dumpster, into Sonja's path.

I knew what was coming. It was always exciting to watch.

Sonja ran through the thing, like she was nothing more than darkness and wind, no substance what so ever.

I had to parkour up the wall. I'm good like that.

Dumb shit had picked a blind alley, he was coming up on a dead end. Not that he saw it. He was too busy staring at the fact that he had just watched the thing chasing him pull a Katie Pride on the obstacle.

He never slowed down as he ran straight into the wall.

He did bounce.

Chapter 7

What's Your Emergency

There, on the ground in front of us, was a man who reeked of death and had managed to do something I had not thought actually possible. He had knocked himself out pulling a Wile E Coyote. I looked up at Sonja.

"Is he dead?" I watched as her eyes went black and filled with star like pinpoints of light.

"**No. But he will be soon if he doesn't get help.**" With that her eyes went back to normal.

I took out my cell phone. After that little display she would have fried hers. Electronics didn't work right when she did that. In the time I had known her, friends had given her three different watches. The record holder lasted a month. She says the record for the shortest was 30 minutes. I asked why, if she knows she's going to kill them, she keeps wearing them. Her answer told me everything I needed to know about her. "They care enough to try. I've told them all and they all think they have found one that will survive me. The least I can do is see if they're right."

While I was lost in my own world of thought as I waited for 911 to connect... nothing. I needed to get further away from her. She was doing the triage thing with the guy. Check breathing, look for injuries, make sure air way is clear, look for head wounds, check pupil dilatation.

"911 what's the emergency?"

"Yeah, this is Claw. I got a man down." I checked the address and gave it to the operator. "He ran into a wall, and his breathing is shallow with..." I looked over to Sonja.

"Rapid pulse, extensive bruising all over. Sluggish dilation."

I informed the operator.

"Alright, help is on the way. Please stay on the line. Is he still in the car and is he pinned?"

"No car, he's laying on the ground in the alley. He's been laid flat and his neck stabilized."

There was silence on the line. "I'm sorry. Is he a speedster?"

"Not unless he decided to go really slow while we were chasing him." I looked over to our friend. I hadn't seen anything special with him, but like two out of every three yahoos in the NYC were powered to one extent or the other. "I don't see any overt signs of the guy being a powered. But I can smell" I took a whiff of the air, opened my mouth slightly and licked. A disgusting bouquet of scents filled my mind, rotten chow mein, pork, and chicken in the dumpster, someone had pissed in the alley, no three different someone's, the smell of cleaners coming out of the now open back door of the restaurant. At least I knew the place was clean. Then, there it was. "He's a tweaker. He's coming down from a meth high."

As I kept a running commentary on the situation, Blade showed up. She took one look at our friend and set up for a football goal. Given how she was cocking back, she intended on going from half field. I grabbed her to keep her from kicking the guy's head like an overripe gourd.

"OY! You fucking wanker!" She screamed at him. "I told her you weren't nothing but trouble."

Sonja came up and took her from me while I was still on the line with the operator. "You know this guy?"

Blade meanwhile was too worked up to answer any questions at the moment. She started verbally unloading on the prick. From what I got, and it wasn't much, Mr. Coyote was an 'old high school friend' of Rayzor's.

By the time the ambulance got there we had a choice, sedate Blade, or she was going to spend some time in a holding cell to calm down. Why? Because she kept screaming how she was going to kill the guy in front of the cops. That alone would have been bad enough, the fact she kept trying and having to be intercepted was the problem. Sonja got them to believe it was a temporary psychotic break. A second ambulance was called and they both went to the hospital.

So much for talking to her any time soon.

"Now what?"

Sonja looked at me. "He was on something, but I don't know what."

"Meth."

She didn't question how I knew, she just nodded. "Someone beat the shit out of him, and not that long ago." She cocked her head to the side. "Something tells me he's not going to sit still."

"So, in other words, our rabbit is going to try for round two?"

She nodded. "Yep."

I grinned at her. "Let's go babysit."

***

Down at the hospital we followed our friend through the system. He was a John Doe for all of an hour. Turns out his name was Richard 'Ricky' Potts, two-bit local hood. Rap sheet was mostly low-level stuff, possession, intoxicated in public, harassment, and a protective order put on him by an old girlfriend. Real charmer.

The cops were sitting on him as a courtesy to us, well, to Kyle really, but they couldn't hold him. Nor could the hospital. He might have been tweaking, but contrary to tv shows, if the cops don't find anything on you, they can't really do much.

That doesn't mean they won't lie their ass off about it.

Which is exactly what they did when he woke up.

"Mr. Potts, it looks like you've had a busy day." said detective Grady. "Given your history, and well, those bruises, not to mention your current condition, why don't I just save you some trouble and call a lawyer for you while we get ready to get you cleared to be turned over to our custody?" He smiled as the guy squirmed. "Or, I can forget the lawyer and the booking, and you can talk to these nice ladies." He let the threat hang in the air. "What's it gonna be?"

"I ain't talking to no cops 'til I get that lawyer. You got nothing on me."

Huh, he wasn't as dumb as he looked. I stepped forward. "Thanks Detective, we'll take it from here."

The cop nodded and went to leave, but suddenly our friend went to panicking. "Wait, you're going to leave me with these two?" He tried to sit upright, but his ribs protested. "No, don't leave me alone with them." His voice was in a complete panic mode now. "I." He seemed to weigh his options, "I know stuff. Just get them away from me." He looked at Sonja, "Especially her."

Some people just had that reaction to her. For her part she smiled at the guy. "I'll wait outside."

He actually relaxed a little bit after she exited the room.

"You going to give me something Ricky?"

"Yeah, sure, just… keep her away from me."

The Detective nodded. "Alright, deal. Now what do you got?"

His mind raced, then his eyes lit up. He had just come up with a plan. "Heard from a guy, the Mexican's are in town. They staying at the shit dive on the other side of the bridge, the one with the smiling sun."

"Really? That's the best you got? You heard?" The detective shook his head, and turned to me, "Nice seeing you again Claw."

"No wait!" The detective stopped, and Ricky, as quickly as he could, pulled up his shirt. "They're there, that's who did this to me."

The Detective raised an eyebrow. "Let me see if I understand this. 'The Mexicans' who are on the other side of the bridge, did this to you?" He nodded. "But you're scared of these two girls." He then shook his head. "You got to give me something better than that. The Mexicans, well that could be anybody couldn't it?"

Tears started pooling in his eyes as they cut back and forth between me and the cop. "Fernández, Rico Fernández."

That got both of our attention. "Rico worked you over?"

But Ricky shook his head. "No, one of his guys did. He watched." He nodded to himself. "I'll, I'll tell you everything you want to know, just, just get me some protection."

The Detective nodded, took out his handcuffs and cuffed Ricky to the bed. "You stay put." He looked at me. "Sorry fuzz ball."

"I know, I know." I held both hands up. "You got a job to do."

As I was escorted out, the cop closed the door. Sonja was leaned against the wall. "Well."

I shrugged, "Snitch just flipped." She rolled her eyes at that. "Part of the deal is we don't go near him."

Detective Grady smiled. "Actually, he just said for me to get you two away from him. So that's what I got to do. Of course, I get off in about," He checked his watch. "Forty minutes, and I suddenly find myself with a lot of paperwork to do. I need to go down and get one of the patrol guys to come up here to babysit him. I think you got maybe, five minutes?"

I kissed the guy on the cheek and went to go in, but he grabbed my arm. "No, I got to make sure you two aren't here, remember."

Nodding we let him put us into an elevator and he hit the L button for the lobby, then let the doors close.

As soon as they were, Sonja hit the floor below the one we were on. "So we need to make this fast. What do we got?"

As we left the elevator and headed for the stairs, I filled her in. "He said the Mexicans got ahold of him."

She nodded as we went up the stairs.

Once back on the right floor we saw that the second elevator was on its way down. Quickly we made our way to the room and slipped in. As soon as he saw us, he started to panic.

"No, no get away from me."

Sonja's eyes did the star thing and she said "Relax, I'm not here for you, we just want to ask a few questions." As she spoke, he calmed down and his eyes grew heavy.

"Really. That's a relief. Ask away." He said in a sing song voice.

Chapter 8

Less than five minutes, still it was creepy when she did this. It was sort of like vampiric hypnotism. The big difference, she told me, is she can't make anyone do anything against their will.

"Ok Ricky." I began, "Let's start from the beginning. Why did you run?" He pointed at Sonja. Well, I did ask. "Let me try another track, what were you doing at the bar?"

"I went to see if that faggot was there."

Oh shit.

My eyes cut over to Sonja, her teeth were bared, her fangs were extended, and they were dripping with saliva. The air in the room dropped a few degrees as her anger grew. There's a reason the vampire lord known as 'The Cat' mistook her for one of them.

In a voice still as sweet as a dream and calm as the sea before the storm she said. "Tell us, why were you looking for them?"

Ricky, unaware of the shift in her mood, answered. "I set the little bitch up with a job, and he's split on me. I was going to either find him, or that slag he hangs out with."

I put a hand on Sonja's shoulder. "What job Ricky? What job did you get her?" I wasn't going to misgender the victim just because this loser did.

"Pick up and drop off. Nothing fancy. Hell, gave him and that fag boyfriend of his a vacation down in Mexico. Stupid fucking slut skipped on me and now my balls are in a vice."

"She was drug running for you?"

"Yeah, I was in a bind but recognized him when I went to the bar. Told him I'd tell his boss if he didn't do what I said." Ricky laughed. "Hell, even got a piece of ass out of the deal."

Ok, that's it. Screw Sonja, I was going to do this dude in. I went to get him and Sonja took my hand and shook her head.

"Is that why those guys are after you?" She asked.

He gave a quick nod. "Yeah, that's a lot of product. If I don't find him and get the shit back soon, I'm dead."

Sonja took and leaned in close to the guy, I watched as his terror slowly won the fight with her calming influence. She whispered to him, and he began to scream.

Not a little. No, I had to flatten my ears he was so loud. So loud, two plain clothes poked their heads inside. One stayed with him, the other kicked us out.

The two of us were escorted completely off the hospital grounds, they all but frog marched us. Mortis was at the corner waiting for us as we got in and drove off.

Sonja was dead calm.

I wasn't. I had heard what she whispered to him thanks to the fact that I'm a cat. "She's already dead, and if you try to run, you will be too. To convince you to do the right thing, have a glimpse of what awaits you on the other side of the veil."

That's when he started screaming.

I would be hearing that sound for weeks to come.

***

By the time we got to the other hospital, I had almost calmed down. I had, she hadn't. As such, it was still colder in her presence than it was outside. I'd have asked her to turn on the heater, but I know she has trouble breathing if she gets too hot. Well, too hot from something like a heater. It was the dry heat that did her in. Wet heat like what we had in Savanah? That she could be in all day and not notice.

We parked, we got out, we went in. Once at the desk we asked for our new friend.

Small problem. "What's the patients name?" The bored desk nurse asked.

"She goes by Blade." I said.

Did you ever have another person just stop and look at you as if you were not only wasting their time, but that you weren't the first to do so, but did have the dubious distinction of being the dumbest to do so?

Yeah, that's the look she gave me. "Are you family?" She proceeded to look me up and down as if daring me to lie about it.

"Um, no?"

"Are you, by chance, part of law enforcement and want to speak to the patient?"

I smiled at her weakly. "Heard that one huh?"

"Hun, I've heard everything you can think of and a few you can't. Now what do you want with this person."

"She's currently my only lead in the case I'm working on."

She blinked at me. "The case you're working on? But you're not a cop."

"No ma'am."

She revised her look for me and let me know that the estimation of my intelligence dropped even more. "What kind of case are you working?"

I took a deep breath, I had one shot at this. "A young trans woman was killed the other night and the police found her and told her mom who hadn't seen her son in five years, and she wants us to find out what happened to her kid and Blade is the only link I have to the child because they were roommates." Yay! I managed that all in one breath.

The look on her face showed that while she still thought my intelligence was a little off, my heart was at least in the right place. "Look, I know who you're talking about, but I can't let you in to see her." I felt my face fall. "What I can do is tell her you're here and if she wants to see you, then I will have someone come and get you, how's that?"

I grinned at her. "Fair enough."

Sonja and I went into the waiting room and, well, waited. I looked around at everyone and some of my good mood dimmed. There were people in pain, men, women, children, all in triage, all waiting to be seen. Most of them were deep into their own world of pain.

Adults, well some adults, have almost an instinctive reaction of fear when it comes to Sonja. Kids? Kids don't have that problem. Kids love her, and she loves them. Soon after we sat down, the two-year-old closest to us, a poor kid who had been bawling her eyes out in her mother's arm, arm, not arms, as the other arm was obviously injured, slowly calmed and started staring at us.

No, not us, at Sonja. Mom was still rubbing her back and the poor kid had the crying hiccups.

Sonja's face went blank, then slowly, her eyes went wide. The kids did the same. Then Sonja blinked one eye, then the other. The kid smiled a little but went back to sniffling. Sonja then slowly started what would become a huge smile. By the time her theatric smile lit up her face, the young girl was smiling, giggling and hiding her face in her mom's hair. The poor woman looked back and saw what, or I should say who had helped, and mouthed "Thank you."

It wasn't long before the two other kids who were waiting, one of them obviously sick and miserable, noticed one of their own laughing. Soon they were all looking at Sonja as she did a very quiet pantomime to keep them distracted.

That's what we did for well over four hours as we waited to hear anything about or from Blade.

Chapter 9

Vengeance

It was six o'clock at night before Blade came strolling into the waiting room. I say strolling because she was walking under her own power, much to the annoyance of the hospital staff. They were still following her in an attempt to get her into a wheelchair.

"I'm damn well fine now aren't I."

"That's not the point miss. If you fall while in the hospital, we're liable."

"Then maybe I'll find a banana peel and we can call us even for the bill and me suing you." As she came in, she saw us. I mean, I'm hard to miss after all. "Oy, you two. Get this," she paused seeing the children, "mother hen off me, would you?"

Sonja went forward, "I have her and take full responsibility." That seemed to satisfy the hovering orderly. While they rolled their eyes at us, they finally stopped following Blade. We took her outside, and the horse, understanding that we were going to need another seat had become a '67 Chevy Impala. Still in the off white pearlescence gray mind you.

"'Ow many cars you two got?" She said as she ran a hand over the perfect lines of the beast. "This is bloody beautiful."

"Careful, you'll give him a swelled head." I said as I opened the door for her. Sonja went around and got in the driver's side.

"Him?" Blade asked.

"The car." Sonja said as she closed her door.

Once settled in, Blade asked as I crawled in and put on my seat belt. "Your car's male?" I shut my door.

"My transportation likes to think of himself as male, yes. I mean, he could probably be a girl if he wanted, but Mortis is male."

<I prefer to think of myself as a stallion thank you very much.>

Blades eyes went wide. "Your car talks?"

<I'm not a car. I'm the transportation.>

I looked back at her. "Mortis is some kind of magical being that has decided he likes Sonja. He can look like anything he wants, which is usually a horse."

As the car cranked up and began to drive on its own, Blade stared in shock. "You got a magic horse?"

One hand on the wheel, looking straight ahead as if she were driving, Sonja got one of those rare smiles of hers. Not one of her creepy ones, or her sarcastic ones, those are a dime a dozen. One of the very rare pride smiles.

I looked back at our passenger, "So two things, where do you live, and what is your legal name?"

She nodded but crossed her arms defensively. "You laugh and I'm out. Got it?" Both Sonja and I nodded. She gave us the address first, then said, "Moira Darling."

I blinked and bit my tongue. An internal struggle went off inside me and required an effort of will that was herculean. Too many movies, too many cartoons, too much pop culture.

Sonja nodded, "Fair enough Blade. I'm Sonja Dec, and that's Claw."

"So how did you two wind up gumshoes?"

Sonja shrugged. "Claw's the freelancer. She's got the paperwork to make sure she is covered legally."

"Sonja helps out, she's got a good mind and sees things."

"I'm riding along with a bloody magical girl and her cat."

Sonja chuckled and we drove on.

Mortis is better than any GPS, and as such he got us to the lovely, overpriced, underwhelming, low grade apartment building. Granted, it wasn't the worst, but it wasn't even midgrade. Blade took us upstairs and let us in.

Well, one thing was for certain, she needed a maid.

"Bloody hell!"

The small space, which was technically a living room, kitchen, bath, and two bedrooms, looked as if it had been ground zero for several teething giant schnauzers. A quick whiff told me that there were old dishes, that someone had been to the gym in the last day, and that this mess was new. Most of what was on the floor was clean clothing. Then I realized that someone had also searched the couch cushions.

"I take it this isn't what you meant when you said mess?"

Blade stopped and looked at me. "Dishes, laundry, not Normandy in my living room." She went to walk in but Sonja put her arm up to bar her.

"Someone tossed this place. You point, I'll go."

"Weird much. Why?"

Sonja stepped in, "Because they left something." She started to look around, as she did her eyes went white.

"I'll tell you what they left, they left a bloody mess is what they left." With that she went to push past Sonja. She made it all of three steps before something shoved her violently back towards me and my now waiting arms.

It saved her life.

In the spot she was about to walk into a trio of black tentacles, shiny and slippery with green ichor, burst forth and lashed out. One lashed itself through the air that Blade had occupied less than a second before. One lashed out towards the couch and as it struck it sliced through the hapless sofa as if it were nothing more substantial than fog. The last of the three lashed out at Sonja.

Blade screamed.

I wrapped my arms around her and twisted to just outside the apartment door.

Sonja hit one knee and looked as if she were bracing herself behind an invisible shield. When the reality ripping thing struck, said shield became visible for a moment. It flickered in and out of visibility as its energies sparked against the black abomination.

While the shield she conjured might not be visible, the sword definitely was. A falchion of light and shadow appeared in her right hand. Shield at the ready, sword parrying incoming attacks, and feet making their way back towards the door, Sonja and the thing put on a hell of a light show.

"What the hell is that?" Blade screamed. That scream echoed in the apartment as the entity's presence warped the fabric of reality around it.

I covered Blade's eyes as well as my own. Whatever the thing was, looking at it wasn't advisable. The sound of the door slamming made me look up, look up and pray that Sonja was on the right side of the wood when it slammed shut.

There, breathing heavy, white eyes wide, Sonja stood. Every inch of her, from stance, to aura, to facial expression gave truth to who and what she was. Sonja was a Celt, a Celt from a long line of warriors who stood between the world and the things that threatened to tear it apart. Part mage, part witch, part priestess, and all warrior.

Unfortunately, she was a warrior with a long black oozing wound on her thigh, a thigh laid bare by the slash of a truly alien tentacle.

Two questions, both spoken at the same time, rang out.

"What the hell was that shite?"

And.

"Sonja, do you know you are hurt?"

She blinked and looked down at the gaping wound, a wound that should be bleeding, but wasn't. Not yet anyway.

"Well shit." She said as she glanced down. "That's annoying." She looked more frustrated than in pain, but that was normal for her. "Grab the girl, she stays at my place till we figure this out."

"The hell you say? I'm..." That was as far as she got before I hoisted her over my shoulder.

That's when Sonja's body caught up with reality and started to bleed.

"No time to argue Blade. You can't stay here, and we have to get her help, now."

Mortis was suddenly in the hallway, he was still the Impala and the bits of him that didn't fit just phased through the wall. I got Blade in the back seat and slid in with her. Sonja jumped into the front. As soon as she was in, the car peeled out and drove. I knew what the landscape was going to look like, to be fair I actually enjoy it. So I saw something as we burned proverbial rubber through a realm I have no name for.

I saw a doppelganger of Blade, only this one was in a rage with tears pouring down her face. It seems Rayzor was not resting in peace. Given the fact that I was pretty sure I now knew who had pushed Blade out of harm's way, it meant Rayzor had figured out how to affect the real world.

God have mercy on those she blamed for her death. She would have none.

Chapter 10

Mortis didn't bother with niceties like roads, or walls, or even ground. Given that, you can guess what he thought of trivialities such as speed limits, and proper parking. The strange world we drove through like a bat out of hell was almost identical to the real world, except for a few minor details. The real New York didn't have thorny brambles everywhere, didn't have a sky filled with swirling dark sectors, and wasn't blanketed in a constant black fog.

Or maybe it did and we just can't see it. The Big Apple was a concrete jungle after all.

We made it to the warehouse in record time and Mortis didn't bother waiting for us to get out. Instead, all three of us were disgorged onto our asses as he just stopped being a car and went back to being a horse. Said horse trotted over to a large wardrobe style wooden cabinet, one with a big lock on it. He turned around, kicked the lock and popped the shackle before turning around and diving into the contents face first.

By the time I had got myself and Blade to our feet, he had already brought a pint-sized jar that had a flickering green living flame inside. Sonja took it from him.

"Thanks horse face."

I turned to Blade. "Come on, you don't want to see this."

"The bloody hell you say. What in the nine hell is going on, what pushed me, and why is my apartment a hentai wet dream?"

Sonja ignored the both of us, she was on the clock.

"That thing was an outer being, I would say they're rare, but they aren't. They are all around us, at all times. The thing is, they aren't on the same frequency as we are."

Sonja ripped her pant leg the rest of the way open and opened the jar. As soon as the contents hit air, a greenish yellow flame leaped forth.

"We should go our entire lives without ever seeing such things, but some 'people' have learned how to shove a small part of those creatures into our world."

Sonja begin pouring the flame onto the wound as if this fire were nothing more than a liquid. As she screamed, I continued to explain.

"Imagine if someone shoved part of you into a two-dimensional space, the beings who lived there would have no clue what they were looking at. But for you, all you would know is that you were stuck to nothing. A hiccup in your movement that made no sense. What would you do?"

As the fire burned, it burned the wound itself off, it left behind perfectly pink skin. Skin, not scar tissue.

Blades eyes were wide as she watched the nonsense in front of her unfold. I asked again to bring her back to the here and now. "What would you do?"

"I'd jerk and try to get lose."

"Exactly. That's what the thing was doing, and in its jerks, it ripped reality the same way you or I would rip paper."

The wound was closed, the fire was out, the jar was empty. Sonja, deep in shock, fell over.

"But her leg?"

"Got folded over so part of the outside was on the inside. It was held that way by the ichor of the thing. She burned that off." The smell of the multi-dimensional blood of the creature now burned away was gag inducing. Sometimes I envy human's sense of smell.

"Now." I breathed in deep. Oh god that was a mistake. I grabbed Blades arm, held my breath and made my way to the door as quickly as my padded little feet could carry me.

Thankfully Blade was done objecting.

Once outside into the stench of a New York alley, with its after dark smells of traffic and humanity living its best life, I breathed deep the normal stench of life, of the real world.

"So, you're saying that thing didn't mean to hurt her, or me?"

I took several deep breaths, then sneezed out the bad air. "I'm telling you; it would have killed you, me, her and never even known what we were. Just that little magots were felt wiggling around its open wound." Fresh air, fresh air was good.

"It was Rayray that pushed me out of the way, wasn't it?"

I nodded. I so needed a bath after that. "Yeah kid, yeah it was."

"What's she going to do?" I looked away. "No, tell me, what is she gonna do?"

"She's a vengeful spirit. What do you think she's going to do?"

"Did she do that?" She made a gesture that might have been towards her apartment.

"No, whoever tossed the place did."

"She saved my life."

"Yeah."

"Is she… is a vengeful ghost evil?"

I shook my head. "The soul is unburdened by the ideals of human morality. Things like fairness are replaced by justice. In that she is far more pure, all pure souls are like that. The problem is, she doesn't know mercy. Justice without mercy is, brutal."

"So, what now?"

The universe hated questions like that. Then again, maybe it loves them. On cue my phone rang.

"Well one, for now, you will stay here." I answered the phone. "Claw's infirmary, you stab 'em we stitch them."

"What the hell did you do to my witness?"

Witness? "Detective. How good to hear from you."

"Don't give me that bullshit, cat. The only reason I'm not hauling you and that dime store psychic of yours down to the station is I wouldn't even have an idea what to charge you two with."

O…K…? "Um, deep breath there chief, what the fuck are you talking about?"

"Potts was screaming for nearly an hour after you two left. By the time he stopped, he started confessing to everything he could think of. Wanted to talk to the DA and didn't want a deal."

I nodded, "I'll tell Sonja you said thank you."

"The hell you will, he just had a massive heart attack about ten minutes ago."

I blinked. Oh fuck. "Is he dead?"

"Thankfully not. But if you or her…"

"Samuel Aaron Smith is a ghost, and a vengeful one at that." Silence on the other end of the line.

"Shit."

"Yeah."

"That's the kid he said he blackmailed into being a drug mule?"

I looked over to Blade, she was listening intently to the conversion. "Among other things." She didn't need to know the guy had raped her friend. I had a feeling that wouldn't go well.

"Yeah, he copped to that to." I heard the man take a deep breath. "How bad?"

"We took Blade home, but someone not only tossed her living room, they boobie trapped it. I suggest no one go there for a while. Anyway, Rayzor pushed Blade out of the way. So, she is still trying to protect innocents."

"That's something. What do you mean boobie trapped?"

"Remember that thing with the thing that Savage got cut by and it took like an hour to heal?"

I heard him whistle over the phone. "So?"

"So, wait till you get a call of shots fired to go there and open the door. That things going to create a big vacuum when it tears itself free."

"Any chance of evidence still being there?"

I thought about it, then remembered the couch. "About the same as either of us winning the lottery."

"How do I keep this guy alive?"

Now that was a question. "Get someone with real faith to put a holy symbol around his neck. Works best if it's his faith but…"

"Got it, anything else? Like salt around him or something, hit it with cold iron?"

Fucking TV. "Cold iron is for fae, though I don't suggest it, and well any crystal that's small enough and enough of them that they reflect energy."

"How about I pay you two to keep him alive?"

I looked back at the warehouse. "Sooner we solve the murder, sooner he's off the hook."

"I'll tell the DA, maybe we can help."

I wasn't holding my breath. "Sure, that works." The window at the top of the place slowly and angrily opened up. She was up and airing the place out. "Talk to you later cop boy." With that I hung up.

I was not going back inside, no way no how, it would be hours before I wouldn't smell charred old ones. Thankfully Sonja came out.

I looked at her. "Buddy boy had a heart attack."

"Shit."

"Yep." I nodded. "Let's go see mom."

"I'm coming too."

I blinked at her and went to object, then nodded. "Can't leave you here with that smell, and you're probably safer with us."

"Too right."

With that Sonja whistled for Mortis.

Chapter 11

Home is Where the Hurt Is

No Impala this time. When Mortis came out Blade asked if he could do any car. As such, well over an hour later we turned up at Mrs. Smith's home in a hearse. To be fair, Sonja loved it. It was a little different from the other vehicles I had seen him turn into, for starters it was actually black. Or more to the point it was the kind of black that the eye skidded off of. Oh, there was still that pale white, sickly gray color, it was just the monochromatic scene that hovered inside that black. A graveyard, ghosts hanging over tomb stones, and Mortis with a reaper on his back.

Sonja turned into a 16-year-old who just got the car of her dreams.

All I could think about was this was so not how to do low profile.

The ride over didn't have a lot of small talk, not that Blade wasn't trying, mind you.

"You guys what, are paranormal investigators?"

I shook my head. "No, we're just two of a small group of weirdos who like helping people out. Each of us has our own way of doing things."

After that she wanted to know who the others were, what they did, and on and on. Given that life had thrown her neck deep into this particular pool, I really couldn't blame her.

A few miles outside of New Rochelle proper we came upon the Smith residence. It was one of a set of larger cookie cutter homes, and to be honest it probably dated back to the white flight of the '50s and '60s in all of its cookie cutter awesomeness. We pulled up, but it was well after nine, and I suddenly remembered humans can be kind of weird about things like strange cars showing up at odd hours unexpectedly. I decided to give Abigail a call.

I watched as someone in the house got up and went to another room, then, "Hello?"

"Mrs. Smith? It's Claw. I know its late, but we really need to talk."

"Have you found out something already?"

"Yeah, yeah we have."

"I, I can come to you."

"Actually, if you look outside, we're already here. I'm sorry, would have called earlier but I kind of spaced on how late it was." Curtains in the house moved and a face was momentarily seen through the glass.

"A hearse?"

"That's us. We found out where your child had been living and got her roommate to agree to come with us. If you're really wanting to know them, I think she can be of some help."

Silence greeted me, it stretched out long enough I got the feeling she was having second thoughts about all this. I opened my mouth to say we could leave her in the car when she made up her mind.

"Come on in." With that she hung up.

As we made our way up to '50s kitsch central, I noticed that the two-story home was exceptionally well maintained. The yard was manicured to within an inch of its life, with the grass, flowers, and shrubs probably too terrified to misbehave. When Mrs. Smith opened the door to great us, her home smelled of fresh cleaning products and air fresheners. Inside, just passed her, it was obvious the place was neat as a pin.

"Please won't you com..." That's as far as she got before she saw Blade. Her mouth fell open and tears immediately started to roll down her cheeks. "Sam?"

For her part Blade looked equally poleaxed. "Bloody hell."

Sonja stepped forward, "Mrs. Smith, this is Blade, your child's roommate. Both of them worked at a bar downtown and, well they pretended to be twins."

"Oy, you look like me mum." The way she said those words, the tremor in her voice, let me know that 'mum' wasn't with us anymore.

"Shall we move this inside?" I made a shooing motion to get the humans moving. People talk about herding cats. But herding humans is much more impossible. Well... until it's not, that is.

As the four of us made our way into Mrs. Smith's pristine home, I became aware of a few things. Despite the freshly clean smell, there was a rotten undercurrent in the air. Second, given the layout of everything, some things were missing. Pictures, most likely, given where they were. Third, the latest cleaning spree had just ended before we got here.

"W- would you like some coffee?" said our reluctant host.

"That would be bangin'." Blade said in a breath. "Why do you look like me mum?" That at least had a little more force to it.

Mrs. Smith tilted her chin up, "I have no idea my dear, but you certainly look like a girl version of my son." She nodded to me, to Sonja and then to Blade. "Excuse me, I'll go get the coffee."

As soon as the woman was out of the room Blade leaned in, "This is too... weird. What the hell is going on?" She pointed towards where Mrs. Smith had just exited, and stage whispered "She's a dead ringer."

"The three of you are in luck, we just got one of those new pod things." Our host called from the other room. "We have a dark roast, French, and a blonde. Which would you like?"

Blade stretched herself, "Miss, I'll do the dark if it ain't to much trouble."

"Sonja wants blonde, and I'll take a dark too."

Sonja meanwhile was looking at everything. I had already noticed there weren't any pictures of Rayzor around from when she had had to be Sam. I wonder if those were the missing pictures. Blade was all nerves at this point, and well, I doubt sitting still was something she was good at under normal circumstances.

As she made her way around the room, she stopped, stared, then picked up one of the pictures and gawked at it. "Bloody hell." She turned back to us. "I know this bloke."

"I'm sorry what?" Mrs. Smith had just walked in with the coffee. Thankfully she had also brought cream and sugar, we were going to need it.

"I said I know this bloke. He's a reg."

Mrs. Smith blinked at her. "I'm sorry, what? That's my husband, Sam's father."

Blade snorted, "No wonder she didn't like him."

"Are you saying my husband… knew where our son was?"

"Well, Rayray kept telling the old fart to feck off. So, I don't know if they had a heart to heart, but I doubt it. But this," Her eyes cut over to the woman. "Sorry, this gentleman was in two or three times a week. Usually he talked to me, but sometimes he talked to her. Always got her back up when he did."

The front door opened as if the opener was pissed at it. Every head turned and looked as a young man, probably in their late teens, stormed in as if the world had pissed him off. On his right hand was a tattoo, 'prison' quality, that said 13 ½, as well as one further up the arm that was an eight ball with two 8s inside it rather than one. His foul mood was accented by the clothing he wore; gold shirt and brown khakis both of which were rumpled as if he'd had a bad night. His head was shaved and he had what a more generous person would describe as a goatee, give it a few years and it would get there. To make the point that this guy was an ass all the more acute, he was yelling as he came in.

"Who the hell parked a body wagon outside, and why the hell didn't you come and pic..." He stopped talking as he turned and saw Blade.

Mrs. Smith stood up and put her hand on her younger son's shoulder. "Edward, this is not your brother."

At that Edward jerked back. "I know that ain't him. The fagot's dead. I just, what the fuck is going on mom?"

"These are the people your father and I hired to look into your brother's death."

At that Eddy boy snorted. "A freak, a pussy, and a Dyke? Stop wasting your money mom." With that he stormed out of the room and went upstairs.

One thing was for certain, Abigail Smith was in hell, and that hell was her own family. What I was not expecting was the look on Blade's face. She looked like she wanted to skin the little asshole.

"I'm getting the feeling you wasn't what she was avoiding."

"I'm sorry?"

Blade looked at Mrs. Smith with a lot more sympathy. "She always talked about how she loved her mum, but she couldn't go back. I didn't even know she had a brother."

Mrs. Smith had had a really bad month in the last ten minutes, and the worst part was, it wasn't over yet.

Chapter 12

"Mrs. Smith." Sonja said as she stood up. "Would you care to accompany us to a local eatery. I am suddenly acutely aware that I have not yet eaten since breakfast." Her voice was calm, quiet. Most people would take this as her working extra hard to be polite. They weren't far from the truth. What this was, was her way of keeping her anger in check.

Mrs. Smith blinked up at her. "I'm sorry?" Then her mind caught up. "I've been saying that a lot." She took a deep breath. "I'm sorry, yes. Let's, let's take this elsewhere." She got up, and went to the base of the stairs, leaned up and went to speak. At that moment the house began to shake with the back beat of music turned up to eleven. The poor beleaguered woman threw up her hands, and grabbed her coat and purse.

We all went outside, us getting into Mortis, her getting into a white Hyundai. We let her pull out first, and we followed. We gave her room, but followed where she went. It didn't take long to realize she was just driving.

"Did you two notice his art?"

I nodded in agreement and Sonja said "I saw."

"Banger of a family this woman's got." Blade huffed. "Son's a fecken nazi, husband's known where Rayray was for well over six months. They treat her like a bloody mushroom."

I blinked. "I don't know that one."

"Keep her in the dark and feed her shit, Claw. Then there's the fact that she looks like your mom. I believe in coincidences, but I don't like them." Sonja looked into the review mirror. "Switched at birth, really are a long-lost twin?"

"Na mate." Then as if a bubble popped. "I grew up in Manchester. Move to London when I was a teen, mostly cuz my da shipped me off to a fancy boarding school." I looked back and could see the tears pouring down her face. "Threw myself in to the locals, learned the slang." She gave a shrug. "I was never really great at it, but I passed. Rayray thought I was the bomb. So, I played it up." She sniffed, "Now she's gone, and her mum looks like me mum."

Sonja nodded. "Even managed to get yourself Asbo trying to fit in." Blade nodded.

"Ok, I got to know." I turned so I could see them both. "What the hell is Asbo?"

"Anti-social behavioral order." Blade said.

"It means she's a menace to society." Sonja added.

Oh, "What did you do?"

At that she grinned. "Tagged the Royal Museum I did. Big time. Put 'house of stolen property' all over the front doors." Then she sighed. "Course, I forgot they got cameras everywhere."

"Ow." London was one of the most surveilled cities in the world.

"My mum had died while I was at school, my dad didn't give two shites about me and what I got up to long as I didn't embarrass him. This definitely did that. So, I figured hop the pond and start a new life." She wiped her face again.

Mrs. Smith, it seemed, had finally decided on a destination and had pulled into an all-night diner. We pulled in behind her and found a parking spot.

Exiting the car, she called over to us. "This place has the best coffee and, well, it's quiet."

We followed her in and all made our way to a booth in the back.

"So..." Mrs. Smith breathed out. "Do you know what your grandfather's name was, or is?"

Blade blinked. "Not really. My dad's da was a big wig with the Tories. Mum's was a right bastard that left ma gran when my mum was just a wee one."

Mrs. Smith nodded. "My dad left my mom when I was a kid. Mother said he had found some foreign tramp to shack up with while he was on rotation in Europe."

Blade blinked. "Buggar. You think my gran was that tart?"

Mrs. Smith, Abigail, was crying again. "I look like your mom, you look, you look like my... my child." Abigail choked back a sob. "Tell me about, her."

Blades face softened. "She was a right firecracker. I was fresh off the boat as they say and lookin' for a place to hang ma hat. We found each other on one of those websites looking for roommates thing. Both of us were absolutely blown away about how similar we looked. She and I got a place. She called it a postage stamp and by London flat standards it was a step down from a palace. She taught me how to be an American, and I taught her how to be British. I had no idea she was, well that she was different. I just thought no one taught her makeup." As she spoke Abigail kept quiet and listened. "She said her mom was great, but a bit of a religious nut. Didn't talk much about her da." She reached over and took Abigail's hand and squeezed. "She was a good girl, helped people out, took care of people. She did what she could and kept me from going down some dark roads. She missed you, but she was scared."

Abigail nodded at that. "Thank you." Taking a deep breath, she looked Blade in the eyes and smiled. "I'm glad she found you, or you found each other." She turned to me and Sonja and opened her mouth.

"Hi. Welcome in, what can I get you fine folks today?"

I swear they have radar. The waitress looked at us all and seemed to either be oblivious to what was going on, or more likely simple inertia kept her moving when she would have rather been anywhere else.

"Coffee black." Abigail said.

"I'll have a little coffee with my cream if you would please, as well as bacon, eggs, and sausage?" The woman nodded at me.

"Can I get a burger and chips?" Again, the woman nodded.

"If I say grits, do you have a clue what I mean?" Sonja asked.

"Oh, I'm sorry hun. We got cream of wheat."

I watched as Sonja shuddered. "Just a cheeseburger and fries please, and a coke."

The waitress winced, "I'm sorry, we have Pepsi, is that ok?"

At that Sonja smiled. "That will get you forgiven for offering cream of wheat."

The waitress laughed, then looked over at Blade. "And what did you want to drink love?"

She thought for a moment. "I could murder an orange pop if you got one."

"Coming up." With that she wandered off.

Abigail looked over at us again. "I, have you found out anything else?"

"Some." Sonja said. "The man responsible for the drugs found on her is in police custody. It looks like he's confessing to everything. However, we think the people who put him up to it are still looking for something."

"I thought the police had already... um, had the um..."

I nodded "They do. But someone went through Blade and your daughter's apartment and tore the place up looking for something."

"Oh." She suddenly got a worried look on her face. "Do you have someplace safe to stay?"

Blade nodded. "Aye, these knuckle heads are putting me up. Trust me, I swear down that I'm safe with these two."

With that Blade and Abigail started talking back and forth, both sharing funny stories about Rayzor, Blade from the last few years, Abigail from the kid's childhood. The food came, as did the drinks and we spent the better part of two hours just listening to what very well probably was a niece and aunt bonding over a lost loved one.

The two of them exchanged numbers and as it was headed to midnight, Abigail decided to call it a night. We all went to our vehicles, and I, at least, was feeling somewhat better about all of this. We had just made it back into the city proper when my phone rang.

"Sex in the city, you got the Kitty."

Silence on the other side for a heartbeat, then. "Miss Claw?"

"Abigail, how goes?" I turned it to speaker phone.

"I just, I..." She took a breath so deep I could hear it over the phone. Then she gave out a sigh. "I want to thank you for all you and your partner have done. I'll write you a check first thing in the morning. Thank you."

Sonja raised an eyebrow.

"Um, we still haven't found out what happened to your daughter, not all of it."

"It's, it's ok. I got what I needed. Thank you for looking into my son." With that the line went dead.

"What the fuck?" Blade said.

Sonja growled.

I knew why. She grew up with this shit. "I'm guessing the husband's home."

"So are you two..."

"No." snapped Sonja. "No, we're not done, not by a long shot." With that she turned into the alley that had the door to her sanctum sanctorum.

Chapter 13

Favors & Bargains

Morning came, and I let myself into Sonja's place quietly. Much to my absolute non shock, I saw that Blade was in the king-sized bed snuggled with enough covers that even I, as a cat, couldn't complain. Sonja of course was at her computer. What was a shock was the condition of the ashtray beside her.

Sonja is a smoker, but an odd one. It's very rare for her to 'need one' and more than two packs a week is unusual. There were exceptions of course. I knew of two things that would have her smoking that much, stress, or sex. Somehow, I don't think Blade and Sonja had been overly friendly.

I walked over, snagging a chair as I went, and sat down beside her. "Pence for your sense?" She grunted and kept staring at her screen. Which wouldn't have been that big a deal, if the monitors were on. "Want to talk about it?"

In a monotone voice she spoke. "I'm out of bale fire. That was my last jar."

Oh boy. "Well, um... Donovan?"

"Already called him. Deal still good."

"Running low on anything else? I mean, he's Sidhe. What's more is he values you, like a lot."

She looked over to the cabinet. "Got plenty of Fairy Fire, short on Hell Fire, but I got to call Michael for that one. I don't keep fel in the house anymore, not after the incident with that rat. Uriel is getting me an entire crate of angel fire."

I nodded, "What about the waters?"

"Haven't needed any but the holy, and I can make that myself." She shook her head. "He may be disgraced, but he's still seelie. I got to be damn careful when dealing with him."

She had a point. "When?"

"Moon rise."

Damn, the old pervert wasn't waiting. "Can you postpone?"

She looked at me. "We're going to need more bale if we run into anymore outsiders."

Shit she had a point. "So, still awake because?"

She looked over at the couch, "I slept. But no. I did some research." She hit her mouse and her screens flared back to life. On it was an 8 ball with two 8s in it rather than one.

"Neat, what is it?"

"They call themselves the peacocks. They bill themselves as an old-fashioned western chauvinist boys club. They swear the 88 is not tied to the Nazis, who they disavow regularly."

"Sounds fun, what's the reality?"

She let out an exhausted sigh, "Great replacement, the erosion of Christian values, erosion of true family values, anti-feminist, men's rights activist, gay fish and frogs." She made a gesture.

"Right, real 'not nazis' stuff there." She gave a shrug. "So, Eddy is a member?"

"Not that I can tell. I trolled the message board, hit the hang outs, even talked to some of the locals. No one has heard of an Eddy, or Edward Smith."

"So, a wannabe's wannabe."

"Yep."

"Anything else?"

"Yeah, turns out Mr. Smith is not only a deacon at the local 'look how oppressed I am' church, but he's also a member of the Promised ones, or was until about five months ago. Turned in his card, or pin, or whatever."

"Hmm, about the same time he started doing some heavy drinking huh."

"Looks like."

I thought about it. "So, no one knows asshole, dad has crawled back into his shell, and mom fired us. On top of that we're fresh out of leads."

She leaned back. "Yep."

"So?"

"So, we wait till Blade wakes up and ask her."

"Ask me what?" Came a groggy voice. "Wait, hold that thought." She stumbled off the bed and into the bathroom.

Ah the morning 'gravity works'. Shortly, she came out and made her way over to us. "Alright, ask me what?"

"Rayzor have any boyfriends?"

"Hit Hadrian's hun?"

I nodded.

"Well," She settled into one of Sonja's oversized, overstuffed thrones. "She had a bloke she dates and one that buys her stuff."

I raised an eyebrow, "She was a sugar baby?"

Blade shrugged. "He treated her well, so I didn't see the problem."

"I don't suppose you have any digits for these men?"

She shrugged and dug out her phone. "When we went on dates or just out for coffee, we always gave the other the name and number of the bloke." She scanned through and gave us two names and numbers. One Derik Shields and one Scott Rice.

"Scott's the sugar daddy."

I looked over at where Mortis was and saw him grab one of the apples that had not been locked up for his own good. "Let's go see a man about a woman."

***

We called ahead, and amazingly we got him and not someone else. Mr. Rice agreed to meet us in person and gave us an exceptionally swanky Park Ave address, the kind we'd have to ride an elevator all the way to the top for. Mortis, of course, easily fixed the traffic problem for us, and deposited us on the building's front steps.

The Doorman nodded as we came up and said, "Mr. Rice is expecting you."

With that we were let in, then a woman met us in the lobby and took us to the private elevator. She put the key code in, then the floor, then left us to ascend the stairway to heaven all on our own.

"Swank."

"Very."

I shook my head. "Ridiculous, if you ask me."

When the doors to the elevator opened, we weren't in a hallway, we were in a foyer.

"Posh."

"Oh yeah."

I didn't have words. Everything was rich mahogany, marble, and, well, nice. I had almost expected this place to be gaudy, over the top, but this was definitely what the kids called style. It even smelled warm, furry, inviting.

An older man, possibly in his early forties, came and greeted us. "I hope you don't mind the inappropriateness, but I got the feeling I didn't want the staff around for this."

That sent Blade's hackles up. "What? Don't want the help knowing ya banging a trany?"

That stopped him. "I would thank you not to use such language in my home please, Blade. My staff are well aware who Miss Smith was. They loved her as much as I did." He nodded. "And I know, given things, you are hurting, so I will excuse the tone. No, that boy she was with? He, you can make that accusation of and be on the mark. As for myself..." his eyes grew wet. "She was supposed to call me when she got home. She called when her flight landed, I offered a car. She declined. I've been dreading this for days."

"Why didn't you call the police?"

He nodded. "I assure you, I did." He nodded. "When I didn't hear from her by midnight, I did. Of course, by then they had other concerns."

"The synagogue fire." Sonja said.

"Quite. As I was not family, I kept getting the run around." He looked at Blade. "I figured you would get to me when you thought of it."

She nodded. "This is Sonja and Claw. They're working the case."

"Ah yes, detectives. I'll be more than happy to chip in with the bill so long as there is progress."

"Well, they just started yesterday and found me, so." He nodded at that.

"So, how can I help, and what has become of my dear Rayzor."

I started. "She was found in an alley after she got back from Mexico."

Blade spoke up. "She told me she was going with you."

He nodded, "Then she lied to both of us. She told me she was going with an old friend. But to be fair she didn't sound happy about it."

"Yes well..." I took a deep breath. This wasn't pleasant. "She had been blackmailed into smuggling something out of Mexico."

His face went cold. "I take it that whatever it was, it was illicit?" I nodded. "Has the charming individual responsible been dealt with?"

"The chuffin' gavvers 'ave 'im."

He nodded at that.

Sonja stepped forward, "Why didn't you..." She seemed to struggle. I knew whatever word she had been about to say had found an express train to fuck off and was long gone. Scott, however, answered her anyway.

"Why did I, if I cared so much, let this happen?" He pursed his lips. "I've been asking myself the same thing. I knew something had happened. To start with I called the hospitals, the cops, anyone I could think of. But all for naught. I, I had thought, she, she was young, and I am not." He nodded to himself. "I thought her worth the wait to be honest. The power imbalance of me having both money and age, and her, well not. I planned..." He reached into his pocket and pulled out a small box. "I've had this with me for two years. In another seven she would have been 30. She was worth the wait."

Great... just great.

"Right now, I don't know how I feel. I had my lawyer drawing her up all the necessary legal documents waiting for her to tell me it was ok to help her with the name change and the other things she needed."

Well, this certainly explained why the hell he was so stiff.

"Do you know who she went to Mexico with by any chance?" Sonja asked.

"Actually, I do." He reached into his pocket and took out his phone. "She sent me a picture of herself on the beach, a couple of them actually. Each time the same young man was in frame." He looked at Blade. "I believe you will recognize the young man."

Blade took the phone and looked. "Bloody hell." She shook her head and handed me the phone. "Derik." Of course, she said the name the same way I said shit after I stepped in it.

Chapter 14

A quick swing through a deli for a couple of bagels and we were off to see Mister Shields. We were taking the traffic route to give the little twit time to answer his damn phone. Seriously, Blade had, 'run him up' several times and got nothing.

"Not that's saying much. He likes to sleep in."

By the time we made it to his brownstone, both myself and Blade were well convinced he was in a coma or had his phone on silent. We headed up the stairs outside and made our way to the elevator. Once on the right floor, my whiskers twitched.

Sonja looked at me. "What?"

I scented the air, then licked the top of my mouth. "Mugwort," I sniffed again, "And pennyroyal." I nodded to myself, "Same as at their apartment."

"Wot about it?"

"It means someone is looking for money." Sonja said dryly. "Stay behind me."

I knew better than to argue, and this time, so did Blade. She pointed the way to our destination, and when we got there, nothing seemed amiss. The door, 1138, was normal looking.

The plants outside were normal looking. The other doors in the hallway were normal looking.

"Looks normal." I said. Look, the more nervous I am the more of a smart ass I am, live with it.

Blade reached passed me and handed Sonja a key from her key ring. "What? She spent the night a lot."

Carefully Sonja opened the door, and revealed a trashed and thrashed pad, same as the girls' place. Unlike the girls' place, this time someone was present when the tentacle bomb went off. The smell of ichor, blood, and bowels was thick in the air.

Blade puked.

So, did I.

Her off to one side, me to the other.

Sonja shut the door, and managed to make it a few steps, before the sound of mine and Blade's lost battles sent her over the edge.

So much for the bagels.

I called our glorious detective.

"What?"

"Get down here, bring a mop, and all your CSI boys. We got a body."

***

By midafternoon the boys and girls in blue had come, and while we still weren't allowed in, Grady was at least willing to talk to us.

"OK. So last night about midnight, we got a call of shots fired from your place." He pointed at Blade. "Dispatch got a call of shots fired from here two hours ago. Cops did a walk through, but nobody saw or heard nothing." He gestured with his pen back towards the apartment. "I'm guessing that's when that one broke free. By the way, the lab boys thank you for not upchucking on the crime scene."

"Sorry." Blade said.

"Her I get. You two? Come on, you two are friends with Kyle, you got to have seen worse."

I looked at the man. "Seen? Yes. Smelled? No."

"What's her excuse?" He pointed to where Sonja was busy going over the outer edge of the door.

"Buckets of blood, bile, and worse. No problem. But everything she sees, smells, or thinks of, she tastes. It's the same way your tongue knows how everything you look at is going to feel."

He went to say something, then ran his tongue over his teeth. "I never thought of that. So, she got to taste all of that?" I jerked a thumb back to the apartment.

"Yeah, but that wasn't what set her off. Us puking did."

He seemed to think about if for a moment, but Blade got it first. "Oh god."

I nodded. "Yep, we might as well have puked in her…"

"That's enough of that. You gonna make me lose my lunch."

"So, what were you three doing here?"

"This was Rayzor's boy toy. He knocked her up regular and we found out he went to Mexico with her." Blade told the nice man.

"We came to talk to him, see if he knew anything." I added.

"I'm guessing he did. It fits, he's got trap pics taped up everywhere around his bedroom." I put my hand on Blades shoulder to forestall us having to bail her out for assault. "Here's a stupid question kitty cat. Why didn't you smell it before the door was opened?"

Actually, that was a damn good question. I smelled the herbs after all. "No clue detective."

A woman clothed head to toe in blue disposable 'don't contaminate the scene' stepped out. "I can answer that one detective." She smiled. "Once the door was closed, whoever did this set a spell up so that sound, smell, and pretty much anything else didn't leak out. Given how some of the runes are inside, I would say someone was perverting Aztec magic to do this."

The detective looked back at her. "Wait, weren't the Aztecs a blood thirsty lot?"

"If you believe the Spanish."

"You don't."

"I think that we'll never know." She smiled at Sonja. "Find anything?"

"No. Just, this door isn't like the others, its newer."

Her, the detective, and I took a quick look at the other doors. "So, what?" He asked. "The bad guy installed a new door?"

"No, this was done months ago." She looked back into the horror that was the living room. "Probably from a break in considering the frame's new, too."

"Alright, so what?"

She looked at the detective as if she wanted to slap him. "So where are the cameras that should be in those mounts?"

The CSI lady smiled. "She's got you there."

"Fine, we look to see if we can find surveillance. Anything else?"

"Dude's a weeb. Probably has more than one computer. One will have all of his personal material on it. That's the one you have to find."

"Yeah, and what are you going to do?"

"Go find the money. Good luck detective."

***

Back down in the car, after we got in, Blade asked. "What's next?"

Sonja looked at the time. "Next, I go home and get ready. You and the fuzzball see if you can find this bruja."

"What's a bruja."

"We talking real Brujeria or asshole?"

"If they are twisting Aztec magic for this, definitely asshole."

"What the shite is a bruja?"

I looked at her, "It means witch."

She slumped back into the seat. "Well no shit, if they are casting spells."

I shook my head. "Lots of different kinds of magic hun. This is mostly likely half understood folk magic mixed with European ideals of morality as well as a wish by the practitioner to be feared." That seemed to satisfy her.

We got back to the warehouse and got out of the car. Once indoors Sonja began to strip. "Hit the computer. We're looking for a motel, probably cheap, in Jersey, with a sun motif." She went over to the shower and turned it on. Turning she gave us a full view of her... bits. "Use my computer. Don't worry about the trace. Dig in. Once you find the hotel, hit that guy of Jess's up. See if he can get us a list of names."

"Spencer?"

"Yeah, that's him. Also hit all the wiccan and pagan shops, see if any outsiders have been buying a lot of pennyroyal lately."

"That and mugwort, good idea, anything else?"

"Yeah, hope I can walk in the morning." With that she scooted off into the shower and I got down to business on the computer.

Blade was blinking at me, "She…"

"Yep."

"But… I mean?"

"Yep."

"Bloody hell." She sat down. "No wonder she's all up in arms over Rayray."

That stopped me. "No, she's like this with everyone." Blade raised an eyebrow at me. "No, really. Sonja has a soft spot for people. She really does. She wanted everyone to live as long and healthy a life as possible. She wants everyone, me, you, Rayzor, the guy down the street she's never met, to live their best life being themselves." I shrugged. "Her default for everyone is this kind of respect love thing, and she gets mad at anyone who fucks someone else over, no matter who they are."

She seemed to think about that for a moment, then asked, "Does it work?"

I looked back over to the bathroom, then at Blade. "I have no idea." I started typing away then stopped. "But you might want to slow your roll on that. One, not only will she likely tell you that you are too young for her. But two, well you will see when she gets back in the morning."

"Like, she has a date, during all of this?"

"No. she has an oath she has to fulfill. From moon up, to moon down, she 'belongs' to a fallen Sidhe Knight of the Seelie Court."

She blinked. "Sidhe... a bloody fairy, they exist?"

"Oh yeah."

Then, more quietly, "What's 'e gonna do to 'er?"

I thought about it. "Enjoy her." It was the best way I could put it.

"Bloody hell...."

I thought about it. Donovan wasn't a bad guy, hell he was a friend and ally. He was also a Sidhe Lord that Sonja had made a deal with. "She'll live. In his own way, I think the bastard loves her."

It took a while, and I typed away like a mad woman trying not to think about the night ahead for my friend, but eventually, she came out of the shower. Her hair was most certainly red now, exceptionally red. She put on furs, knives, a head dress, all Celtic. She was heart stoppingly beautiful, even to me. She looked like she came off some '80's album cover, or something painted by Vallejo himself.

I knew she was in for a hell of a night.

"Keep me posted. Call Mortis if you need him. I'll see you after moon down."

With that, she opened a door in the wall that, until moments before, hadn't been there and walked in.

I shuddered when it closed.

Chapter 15

Blade looked at where the door was, then to me, then back to the blank wall. "So, this happen often?"

I shook my head. "Every full moon."

"And that door... is it like what I saw when we were driving through everything?"

"Yes and no. Yes it's like it, no it's not the same thing." I turned the chair and got back to the computer.

Blade came over and took up residence in the chair I usually rest my rump in. "So, what's her deal?"

Sooner or later, all the normies ask. "Before I answer that, could you define what you mean by what's her deal?"

"She just seems odd is all."

I looked over at Mortis, who I swore was silently laughing, then back to her. "Wait, you think the woman with the magic horse, who as we speak, is lacing up her boots to do the horizonal mambo with an honest to god elf lord, who created a shield and sword out of nothing to defend all of us from Cthulhu's wet fart is odd?" I looked at her and smiled. "Say you don't mean it."

She then actually punched me in the arm. "I'm serious. She doesn't have to be here. She has a magical horse, is a bed partner with a fae, and is obviously magical. So why is she still here, still," she gestured around at the mundaneness of the place. "Here?"

Ok, that was actually a good question. "Most people just want to know why she's odd."

"I'm not most people. I'm not sure I would be hanging around Mundanea if I was one step away from being a fairy tale. I'd choose the fairy tale every time."

I stopped typing and turned to her. "I asked her the same thing shortly after I met her. I'll tell you the same thing she told me. You'll either get it, or you won't."

"Fair enough, shoot."

"Imagine that you were a great swimmer, not a good one, but a great one, we're talking Olympic gold good. Then you saw an entire bus load of kindergarteners go off the road and into a swift river. She, and I'm paraphrasing this part, would jump in even if she could only save one or two. She would keep going back until she either dies, or all the kids were on dry land." I looked at her intensely. "Now imagine someone with that same dedication, but who was only an ok swimmer. That's Sonja." I turned back and went back to typing.

"That's… Actually, I don't know if that's the best of ideas. Doing that would mean that a better swimmer would have to save her as well."

I smiled as I typed away. "Good logic, I said the same thing. Her response, 'We don't wear indicators of how well we swim. While I wait to find our if there is someone who swims better than I do, lives are lost.' Then she smiled at me and said. 'The best option would be if I weren't the only one jumping in, but I'm not waiting to see who joins me.' I've been jumping in with her ever since." Bingo! "Got it. Morning Rise Inn, just off the turnpike. Its sign is a rising sun."

"Blindin'. So wha now?"

"Now, I hope Spencer is taking requests." I shot off an email in his direction, it read. "PC and Dark Rider need 411, contact asap."

Blade looked at me funny "So who's Spencer?"

"A friend of ours computer expert. He's kind of a do all kind of guy."

"A hacker."

"More or less."

"Let me guess, they call us?"

I pointed at the web cam that had suddenly come on, came on without it popping up. "He's already here."

A DOS style black window opened, when it did, a simple sentence was displayed.

::Who's the civilian?::

I smiled and waved enthusiastically at the camera. "Hihi, this is Blade, she's the client."

::Right. Hi C.L.A.W. Seeing as this isn't your computer dare I ask where Sonja is?::

"Indisposed."

::I don't want to know?::

"You really don't want to know."

::Fine. What can I do for you?::

"I got a place that I need to find out who is staying there. I'm looking for Mexican nationals, possible fake credentials, and I need it soon."

::Soon or ASAP::

"Soon is fine."

::I take it the motel you have up on screen::

"Yep."

::I'll see what I can do, no promises. I'm busy.::

"Na, we good."

::Goodbye C.L.A.W.::

With that the whole computer rebooted.

"That sounded fun."

"Eh, Jess trusts him."

"Ok, what does that mean?"

I thought about it for a moment. "That he's as safe as anyone can be. Jessica doesn't trust people easily."

"Noted. So do I get to meet this, Jess?"

"You better hope not. She specializes in making people disappear."

"What, like a hitman?"

"No, like witness protection."

"Oh, yeah no. Let's avoid that." She looked around. "So, what now?"

"Well, we could play twenty questions, or we could play twenty questions."

"What's the difference?"

"Who's asking the questions of whom?"

"I can ask anything?"

I thought for a moment, this could be fun. "Of course, though there are some questions I just can't answer."

"Because they are personal?"

"No... because of the Heisenberg uncertainty principle and the fact I can either tell you velocity or location... Well, not really, I can't do the math, so that's two sets of questions I can't answer."

She laughed, "Are you always this much of a smart ass?"

"Yeesssss!"

"So, why don't we go back and forth. I asked one, you're turn."

"Great." I spun around to the rebooted computer, popped open a tab, hit the search engine and typed in 'Local shops that sell pennyroyal', and waited.

"Oh..." Blade sounded disappointed. "I forgot you needed to check on that."

"Yes, but you name it a fun game. Your turn."

"I thought maybe you were going to ask me something?"

I nodded, "And I will, that's part of the fun." I spun back around and clicked open the first link. There it was, the number I was looking for. I called, asked, and found out no one new had come in and bought any. "Your turn."

"Ok, so how often do you guys deal with those tentacle things?"

"Not often, and no I don't really understand them either, but they aren't the weirdest thing we've run into." I hit the second shop and got the same results.

"So, what is the weirdest thing you've run into?"

"Oh, that one is easy. There's a guy who lives in the park. Nice guy, but he claims to have an invisible dog. Turns out he did, sort of. The 'dog' in question was indeed invisible, but it was less a dog and more a human who preferred to be a dog. We found them when the guy hired me to find out who kidnaped his dog. Turns out it was this guy who thought having an invisible dog would help with doing crime stuff. Dude had no idea dude was a dude, but neither did the owner. Finding the mutt in question we found out that not only could the 'dog' talk he could stop being invisible and was scared if he told the crime guy the truth that said crime guy would shoot him."

I then hit the next one on the list, nada.

Blade blinked at me. "You're serious?"

"Yep." I checked the next one and got a hit.

"Actually yes, a woman came in the other day and bought everything we had when it came to pennyroyal. She said someone had stolen her entire stash while she was working with a customer. She's not one of my usuals."

"Great, can I get an address?" I quickly wrote down what she told me. Hanging up, I looked at Blade. "You get two now."

"Ok, so that was the weirdest, what was the scariest?"

That stopped me cold. "Um, a friend of ours had a daughter, she got kidnapped by a cult. I've never been more terrified than I was helping to look for that poor kid." My mind went back there, back to where we found her, how we found her. "It's one of the few times I've actually seen Sonja pissed. She was cold, quiet, and... she was a force of nature." I swallowed. "Come on, we can talk more on the way..."

"Where are we going?" She got up.

"To go see a psychic." I nodded to her. "How do you feel about motorcycles?"

"I've always wanted to ride one."

I grinned at that, as I took her hand and led her outside.

Chapter 16

Big Red Button

There are few things in this world that I am attached to and proud of. Being ex-military, even if it's an interesting kind of ex, my firearms are of course on that list. But a gun is a gun and if need be, my beloved tools of destruction can be replaced. My bike cannot.

One day I was watching this show, don't remember what it was called, but it was all about custom bikes. I saw what they did and I fell in love. My training included how to strip down any American engine and rebuild it if necessary, I was sure I could make me a Cat Custom Chopper. So, I got the engine I wanted to build it around; a twin cam 88, and proceeded to spend the next three months trying to rip my hair out.

I was a grease monkey, sure... but fabrication? Not my strong suit.

That's one of the reasons I love Sonja so much. Her dad taught her how to weld, grind, and shape metal. Her and him didn't always get along, but when it came to teaching her stuff, the guy was stand up as hell. She came in to check on the monstrous amount of noise I was making and just started helping. I didn't ask, she didn't offer.

Once my engine was freed from the pile of junk I had deluded myself into believing would be a bike frame if I just tried a little bit harder, I told her what I wanted. She listened, nodded, asked questions, and then said. "Close your eyes and picture your bike. It's done, it's perfect. Tell me what you see." I must have gushed for an hour. By the time I was done, I could see her, mirrors to exhaust. It took her a month, but she delivered.

My baby, my darling, my sweetheart, was a chrome covered necromancer version of a Smilodon skeleton where the front paws held the front wheel, the back held the rear, and the bit in the mouth led out to chains that became the handlebars. She purred like a kitten, and roared as loud as I do. After I did a job for a gear head mage I am friends with, she got an upgrade in the form of a red 'push me' right at what would be the nape of my ancestors' neck. I maybe could get another bike, get the same modifications, it might even be identical, but the truth was? She was my Mortis.

Utterly irreplaceable.

It also helped that my other baby, my old service rifle, was taken apart and hidden within the natural and unnatural lines of my wonderful bike. I had given Blade a helmet, gotten my own, strapped on the sisters and my jacket (black leather of course) and we hopped onto my beauty.

It did my heart proud when Blade saw it and said, "Now that's a bike."

Once she was up and purring, and shaking fun parts of me, I pulled out and started heading to the psychic's shop.

"OK." Blade's voice sounded in my ear. "How in the hell did you get this beast?"

"Sonja." I said back. "Got the helmets from Jennifer, so yeah we're going to be able to hear each other quite well."

"So, you too been together long?"

"Yeah, I've known her for almost ¾ of my life now. No idea how old I will live to be. Downside of being a lab rat."

"How old are you now?"

"Hey, that's three." I pulled out into evening traffic. "22, and my turn. So, real reason you two did the twins thing?"

Silence greeted me for a while. "My mom's dead, and my dad's an ass. I think we both wanted family."

"I can see that. Any idea what you're going to do now?"

"Well, I forgot to call in today, but it probably doesn't matter. Boss knows what's what and he'll probably cut me some slack." I felt her shrug behind me. "Probably go back to work." Her voice was sad at that.

"How much wood, could a wood chuck chuck, if a wood chuck, could chuck, wood?"

The silence behind me stretched out. "Do you joke about everything?"

"I'm a test tube baby made to be a disposable soldier. It's laugh or have an existential crisis every day. Actually, I had one of those already, and decided to use my humor to help people. Point out where they are taking themselves too seriously, need to pop an ego or two, that kind of thing."

"Must be nice to have a purpose."

"I was born with one of those, it's nice to choose my own." As we road along, we started bantering back and forth and I realized, Blade had a wicked sense of humor. Took a bit of start, stop, slide, and squeezing, but eventually we got where we were going.

Sadly, it was in Jersey. Nothing's perfect.

Madam Aponia, Palmistry, Tarot, Birth Charts. Open at sundown, closes at midnight. Behave within my walls, the spirits are watching.

Blade was not impressed. "Gee, class place this, ain't it."

"It's aces. Come on, and be careful. She could be the real deal and playing it up for the rubes."

"What like a real psychic… which given what I've seen so far isn't that bonkers. So, never mind."

We went up to the place and the door opened as we got there. As I walked in, I could see the trigger mechanism for it, though to be fair it was well hidden. The place might well have come off a low budget Hollywood backlot set. The kind where cheap was the name of the game as long as it got the right idea across. A middle-aged white woman wreathed in what could only be called fake gypsy scarves flowed into the room.

"Hello and welcome, I am Madam Aponia, and you," She looked at us, "Are not my 8 o'clock." She cocked her head and looked at me and Blade, then in a tired voice. "She's got a ghost, you got a soul, and your friend is going to be fine. Anything else? I got to get ready for the Goldstein's."

"Bloody hell."

"Actually, I knew all that." I went to say more but she beat me to the punch.

"Well, someone didn't, that's what's been screaming since you two came in."

Blade made a face. "Sorry, I'm new at this."

"Fine, what do you want kitty cat?"

"Don't ya know that too?"

"Don't be smart kid. I can barely hear her over you." She squinted her eyes at me, "Can't hear you at all actually."

"Look, you recently bought the entire stock of pennyroyal from Five Shards."

"Yeah, what of it?"

Psychic? Check. From Jersey? Check. "Who stole your old stock."

"How the hell should I know. I was helping out this cute tourist couple when my door opened. I thought one of my regulars had stopped by. It happens. So, I'm working the fake stuff cuz these two were about as interesting as a Fragile Lamp Shade, if you catch my drift. He didn't love her; she was thinking of another guy. The usual. So, I'm spinning them enough what they want to hear to get a fat tip, and boom. They're gone. But so is my entire stock of dried pennyroyal. My money charms are my best seller."

"Didn't happen to lose any mugwort when it happened?" Blade asked. Smart girl, she remembered.

"Matter of fact, yeah. Not only that, they cleaned out all of my fulgurite as well, even my big one. Got an insurance claim on that one."

"Why didn't you buy more?"

"What for? Stuff mainly sells as a curiosity. Not a lot of call for frozen divine fire for what I work with. And no, I got no interest in anything but the tourist stuff." She shrugged her shawl back onto her shoulders. "I got no interest in getting back into real magic. That shit's dangerous. Now if you don't mind." She gestured behind us where a car was pulling up. "I get to lie to a nice wife about her dead husband. So, if you don't mind."

As we went to go out, Blade spun around and asked. "So, the couple, where were they from?"

"Mexico, I think."

Damn, I liked this girl.

Together she and I walked out to my baby.

Chapter 17

Donuts & Bad Dogs

I handed her the helmet and wrapped my thighs around the frame waiting for her to get on. Look, I'm a one-of-a-kind creature, my ride is my only ride if you catch my drift. Humans just don't do it for me. As for real tigers? Talk about himbos. All looks and zero brains. I need something, someone, I can have a conversation with.

"Where to?" She said in my headset as she got on.

"Well, we're going to go to the motel next. Not much else we can do at the moment. Maybe we'll get lucky. Who knows, maybe they'll order Mexican. They got to eat." She nodded and away we went.

The motel in question was in, well near, Hoboken on 78. To call it a dive was to do dives a disservice. The good thing about it was the Dunkin across the street. We turned in, got doughnuts and coffee, some snackin' bacon, and set up in the dark, dead end alley across the street. The place was set up as a single-story horseshoe courtyard that had a pool at one point in its life. Said pool was now a rock garden. The lone ice machine was next to the office and the almost defunct coke machine sat in all its decaying glory right by it.

There were half a dozen cars and trucks in the parking lot, as well as two vans. Most of those cars boasted out of state plates. One of the trucks, both vans, and three of the cars had New York plates, the kind used for rentals. This was the place, it had to be, but there was no guarantee they were still here.

"You do stake outs a lot?"

I snorted at that idea. "More than I like. I'm licensed, but not a real private eye. I mostly do a combination bounty hunter, cheater catcher gig." I sighed. "The second part is not my favorite. But lawyers hire me when things get either really bad or really stupid."

She gave me a snort, "Define stupid."

"Well, one time," I couldn't stop myself, "At band camp, I was paid to find this guy that went missing once a week, every week same time, but always from different places. The lawyer needed to know where he was going and if it had anything to do with the missing money from his company. Had to get Sonja's help with that one. Dude was banging a working woman who was part elf. She kept pulling them into a side reality. While she did the do, her partner used the company credentials to get in, but always made it look like it was someone else. The team had made off with about half a mil before anyone put together it was always at the time dude was missing."

"Ow, what happened?"

"The working woman was just told to keep her client busy and happy. She had no idea she was being used."

"Bet she still went to jail."

Sadly, she was right. "We've got another lawyer friend trying to get her out."

"Fun."

"Not really."

We sat like that for a while, in silence. I had no idea what to say after admitting I had got a poor woman locked up. The two of us watched, waited, drank coffee, and ate doughnuts. The night was somewhat chilly, so I took my jacket off and put it on Blade. I had fur, the human didn't.

Minutes turned to hours, one cup to three. Blade did the running since she didn't see as well as I did. Slowly but surely we got into a rhythm. She was coming back with coffee four and some crullers, when I realized her gait had changed.

I glanced over at her and saw she was stiff, shoulders back, eyes straight ahead, box of doughnuts and coffee bared before her like the king's royal cloak. She was trying for nonchalant, and failing. She came over, eyes wide, and handed me the box.

"Oh, my god." Her breath was short, and her eyes were wide with fear. "So, this guy just came into the shop as I was going out. He was talking to his friends in Spanish and did a double take when he held the door for me." She put the food and drinks on the impromptu table we had made with milk crates.

I nodded, and motioned with my head for her to get on the bike. "Don't panic. I got you." I reached up to the heat in my arm pit and clicked it free but left it in the holster.

I kept my ears picketed as nothing happened. Then, all of a sudden, nothing kept happening. Couple of things to know when you're a highly trained predator, nothing happens far more than something. If you let all that nothing lull you into thinking nothing will keep happening, you're caught off guard when something does happen. So, when someone walked up from behind us, I wasn't surprised.

I should have been, it was a blind alley. Logic dictated; nothing should come from behind me. But then, I work with a person who can literally ghost through walls. My familiarity with that saved Blade's life.

The shot wasn't loud, that meant the caliber was small, and I had a choice when I felt someone behind us, commit a sin, or let them do whatever they were going to do. I decided I would apologize to my baby later and dumped her to the ground as I started her up and got us out of the line of assholishness. The sound of metal scraping the concrete of the sidewalk broke my heart.

The headlight of my grinning saber tooth tiger flooded the alley behind us. What it illuminated let me know a few basic things. First and foremost, that pop hadn't been a gun shot. That pop had been the second thing, the mage stepping into existence behind me. The guy had to be in his 40s, and his mode of dress was immaculate. He was style, he was grace, and he so wanted to rearrange our face. The last thing was the thing between us and him. It was, well it was a Dark Hound.

Dark Hounds do not look like dogs, not unless your dog walks on its hind legs comfortably while its front legs were held straight up as if it were surrendering. Oh, and they need to have huge, clawed hands instead of paws. Add into that the two skinny, rope-like tendrils that ended with grasping little four toothed mouths, and a head best described as a Tetrahedron where each side has an eye at the vertex and a mouth that opens at the apex to reveal a cone of throat teeth. Needless to say, such a creature was not meant to be in this reality, and reality quite agreed with you and I on this point. So, it looked as if the air around it was trying in vain to push it back through the nothing it had been summoned from.

Now, if you are at all a sane person, you're probably asking why it's called a Dark Hound if it is not in fact dog shaped. Simple my friend. They are trackers. The only good news here is unlike the tentacle fest we'd dealt with so far these things could technically exist in our reality, just not comfortably. That meant it was here, and here meant I could touch it.

Or more importantly my bullets could touch it.

I cleared leather with the firearm I had already popped loose and proceeded to pump five of my .45 caliber friends right into its opened maw.

'Not a good boy' fell over.

The mage, I think, was rather surprised.

"I have never seen someone shoot one of my pets before." He said in a thick accent. "But again, I assure you, I have also never seen a tigre riding a motocicleta before either. So, it is a night of firsts. In that I will give you this chance, but only this chance. Give me the Puta so she may tell me where her boyfriend has hidden our posesión, and I will not have the rest of the pack" he spread his arms wide and ten more Dark Hounds came out of the shadows, "harm such a truly unique creature such as yourself."

I smiled. "I don't suppose it matters if I tell you, that this is Blade, not Rayzor would it?"

That stopped him, "Why would it?"

"Different people chief. Rayzor's dead." That stopped him, "Cops got her body, your drugs are long gone."

He blinked. "I do not care about the drugs." His words were angry, "I want what her boyfriend stole from me."

He was talking, but I was lost. "I don't know what that is, and again, this isn't Rayzor, it's Blade."

He nodded. "Rayzor, Blade, whatever. She knows him, and he will, I think, do the right thing once we have her. Now, pretty little gato, please to be handing her to me."

"No."

"Pity, bring me the girl my pets."

The hounds started to move, but I didn't wait to see. I hit the gas and peeled out. "I hope you can hear me hun." I said as I headed for the closer on ramp to 78. "But you need to hold on tight."

In response, she tightened her grip around me and molded herself into my back. I risked a look behind us to see that even though I had made it onto the freeway and was really opening her up, the hounds were gaining.

I checked to make sure we had wide open road, and realized we were going west. It couldn't be helped. We needed to put as much distance between ourselves and the hounds as possible.

I said my prayers, and hit the big red no-no button.

I am, in my heart, a geek. So, when a mage said he owed me and wanted to return the favor, I asked him to supe up my bike. Oh boy did he.

As the button was fully depressed, flames shot out of the eyes of the skull, the wheels caught on fire, and my bike roared. I went from almost 100 mph to warp speed. The only reason I could do this is because kitties have super reflexes. God only knew how fast we were going, I didn't dare look down at the speedometer, not that it went that high anyway.

What should have taken an hour took minutes as we made our way to Greenwich. The button clicked off before we hit the town proper. The good news is it was only made for us to go about 50 miles at a time. The bad news was, I now needed gas. It never mattered how much I had in the tank, when the ride was over I only had enough to get me to a gas station.

Slowing down, I made the exit and went looking for fuel.

Thankfully I hadn't lost Blade. By the time we got to the gas station I realized I would need to pry her off myself very carefully.

Chapter 18

Siege Them

Once I parked the bike, and gave my poor passenger a moment to collect herself, I got off and popped the tank open. Flipping the cap off I handed the whole thing off to the attendant. Got to love New Jersey. I looked back at Blade who was still hugging herself. "Want me to get you a pop or something?"

"Are we safe?"

The attendant had been doing a decent job of ignoring us up until that point. "You twos need help?"

I shook my head at him and her. "Those things have our scent. We got away from them, but they will track us down."

The guy, who, well he was human but he looked like a teen still, started to shift uncomfortably as he finished the tank and went to take a step back.

"Relax kid." I gave him my best smile. "We're being chased by a mage who has sent extra-dimensional hounds to drag us back to him." I watched as his eyes got huge as my words sank in. Then, at the height of his trepidation, I wiggled my eyebrows.

He gave a snort, "Had me goin there for a sec. You two be safe out there." With that he walked back to the warmth of the inside.

I took the moment to check the moon's position. 20 degrees past apex.

"If those things can track us, what are we going to do?"

"Well, we're going to lead them on a merry chase to start with. They can be fast as hell, but only in bursts. They are made much more for endurance. If we wait here, we got maybe two hours." I nodded to myself. That felt right. "But what we're going to do is swing wide and head back to the city. Sonja's place is warded, well for obvious reasons. Once we get there, we'll figure out or next move."

She nodded as I got back on, then asked. "Are we going ta go that fast again?"

"We should avoid it if we can." I looked at the front tire. It wasn't bald, but it definitely needed to be swapped out. "Doing that is hard on my baby." She got back on, and we started off again. I took 611 over to 80, then turned back towards the city.

I kept an eye on the moon the whole time. I didn't know if those things could catch up with us, if they could get ahead of us, or really anything more about them than the bare bones basics. They were fast so they could go in for the kill. They weren't persistent predators like humans were, but like wolves they could almost keep up. I knew that much because I came up on the aftermath of a 'hunt' once and kind of freaked out on Sonja wanting to know what the hell had done that kind of damage.

She told me all she knew, including the fact that if you gift them with enough high velocity copper coated lead, that you could in fact kill one. That made me feel better. The question was, what kind of mage had eleven of the damn things tagging along. Not to mention what the hell was he looking for? It took us a little over two hours to get back to the city. Needless to say, moonset was still hours away.

We pulled into the alley, and I went around to the old loading dock. We had installed a ramp so that, if needed, my bike or someone's car could be squirreled away inside. I hoped off the bike, helped Blade down, then opened the place up, letting us in.

"Mortis!" I yelled into the darkness. "How do we..." I stopped dead in my tracks. I mean come on, what else was I supposed to do?

Sonja was back, way early. Which, hey, should have been a good thing, if not for a few minor details. One, she was naked, two she was laying face down on her bed, three her body was covered in rope burns and bruises, and four, she wasn't alone. Indeed, one of Donovan's girls was there with her, unglamoured.

Unfortunately, Blade had also seen the woman. Elf struck is real. To be fair, the Sidhe are a bright, shining people. Their skin isn't pale, it's damn near white, what's more is it glowed. That glow is what gave them different types. To be honest, it meant about as much as Race did in terms of them being different. Unfortunately, there were Sidhe that viewed such minor differences the same way humans do. The young lady before us was glowing ever so slightly silver.

To top everything off, she also looked pissed.

At me.

What the hell did I do? Well, besides lead Dark Hounds here... did she know about that yet?

"Cat, when is the last time The Mistress slept?" That voice of hers was pure music. The tone transformed it from a light airy aria to a dark one.

I blinked at her. "Um, at least two days." Then I started racing around and closing things up. "Mortis we need to get the wards up, like all of them." The horse didn't argue, he just started moving. "It's possibly been longer than that, but I'm honestly not sure. She told me she got some last night."

"What did you do to her?" Blade's words were barely a whisper.

The Sidhe blinked, "Me? I massaged her feet, perfumed her and got her ready. I didn't get to play with her this time. Then Master Donovan bid me take her home and see to her." She turned back to me, her gaze following as I scurried along. "What ails?"

"A mage has sicced Dark Hounds on me and the girl."

The woman stood up; outrage poured forth from her. "And you brought the foul things here?" Her question demanded an answer.

"The young lady is under Sonja's and my protection." With that I got the last of everything closed up. "Don't take this the wrong way, but why are you... why is she back early. I didn't think it worked that way."

Blade stood transfixed at the level of damage that seemed to have befallen Sonja. "Is she ok?" With that she met the Sidhe's eyes.

The woman looked over, and began to answer us both. "She is fine, though I fear she may be disappointed. She actually fell asleep during the scourging. Master said she must have been beyond exhausted."

"She fell asleep while being whipped?" Blade's voice cracked, punctuating her disbelief.

I looked at the poor girl. "Like I said, you may want to see what she calls fun before you set your mind to the idea of her. So, the Big D sent her home, huh?"

She raised an eyebrow at that. "He did, though I think he may take issue with the familiarity. I am to stay with her for the rest of her time, to see to her needs." The woman pursed her lips. "We expected not an incursion. A moment." She quickly walked over to a mirror and spoke into it. "Master, there has been a development. We are about to be besieged by Dark Hounds. The Mistress is well and truly sleeping. I beg your permission to wake her."

Blade had finally torn her gaze from the happily sleeping Sonja, and looked at me. "Why would she be disappointed, and um, why is she asking permission to wake her up. Shouldn't we just?" She mimed shaking someone.

"We try and she'd stop us. No, under their deal, until the moon sets, Sonja is Donovan's property. That means he has to put her needs first. It's part of their deal. What's more is fun time isn't supposed to interfere with her job."

The nowhere door opened again, and a litter was brought forth with a stricken man who glowed slightly orange, carried by women who were silver, orange, gold, and green. Donovan had arrived. Blade and I both stared. He had that effect on people. As the litter was set down, the emaciated Sidhe stood. Doing so obviously took its toll. Too skinny, too frail, Donovan was under a curse, one that wasted him, but would not let him die. His hair cascaded down his back, and despite his infirmity, his eyes glowed with pride and power.

"Master, you..." That was as far as the young lady got before her master stopped her words with a glance.

"I am the only Seelie she trusts. Think I wish to change this? I will stand while she cannot."

The woman's chin went up and her demeanor changed. "Listen here, what do you think she will do when she wakes and finds out you pushed yourself this hard? Do you think she won't beat herself within an inch of her soul once more." She took a breath. "Let me wake her."

Donovan shook his head. "The Tiger is here, as well as an old line. I need not armor up for this siege, merely direct it." He sighed. "Don't worry Betha. I won't overly push myself. As I said, I am the only Seelie she trusts. I will not jeopardize that, myself, or her friendship." He managed to stay tall as he walked to her. "Besides, I picked of your sisters, my best warriors."

Betha gave him a pout, then nodded. "So you did. Promise me you will not armor."

He gave her a sad smile. "I promise you, and her, I will armor only if necessary."

She took his hand and kissed it. "That's the best I'm getting, isn't it?" He merely nodded. She turned, looked at her 'sisters' then barked. "To arms!"

Chapter 19

Five armor clad sidhe warriors later, the big man was barking orders. Each wore a set of plate that was all artistic beauty and deadly grace. Each pulled blades free from scabbards and readied shields. Part of me was kind of giddy seeing their swords, after all the falchion was my favorite sword.

The four took a compass point, while the last went to cover Donovan himself. He, however, looked at her and raised an eyebrow. "Stand over your charge, I've not changed your orders."

She looked at him, then towards the bed. "Cat, will you hand me that chair, the one with the wheels by the desk?" I slid the desk chair over to her. "Sit, and I will watch you both. Argue and waste time."

With a pout he sat down in the chair. "Who exactly is in charge here?"

With a smile, she wheeled him close to the bed. "You are, of course, dear Master." She then gave a sigh, "But you and The Mistress are equally stubborn. Neither of you will look after self if there is so much as one other to see to."

Watching a several hundred-year-old knight pout at a woman who called him Master did my heart a world of good. Blade walked over and looked at him.

"You're not exactly what I was expecting."

He gave her a smile, "That my dear, I will take as a compliment."

"Can I," She stopped and thought about her words. "May I ask you more than one question?"

Donovan's laugh was rich, deep, and full of humor. "Oh, you are a wonder. Yes, ask anything you wish, I will not hold it against you."

She looked at him, the girls, and then Sonja. "I don't understand what's going on here."

The warrior nodded, "Not precisely a question, but I know what you mean. You see, I abuse the old slave, cast, and indentured servant system. Each of my many servants were, let's say treated poorly by their former positions. I take them in, bind them to me, and in doing so take on their debts. I quickly pay those off or defer them. We're a family you see, they look after me, and I after them."

The woman, Betha smiled. "We also take care of other needs we have. While our lord may be sinister, his rank is still far too high for any in the court not to honor his agreements."

"As for her?" Donovan lovingly looked over at Sonja. "She is in a pain few can understand. She should have spent her life well spoiled. Instead, she has become hard." He looked at me. "How long this time?"

"Like I told her, I know of at least two days. But if she, well."

"Indeed."

"We're working a case, I was hoping it would get her mind off, whatever."

He nodded, "We got her tied, stretched and I was just getting a rhythm when... well I realized though she was still very much enjoying herself, she was not awake."

Blade raised an eyebrow at that. "Her back is in ribbons, she enjoys that?"

Both of them laughed. "See for yourself girl. The bruising is superficial and must be magically induced. She doesn't bruise easily. Even this will only last a day, two at most." Blade walked over and inspected Sonja's back. "I deal with fantasy my dear, with illusion, with the seeming. There is enough truth in the pain to let her forget herself, but there is no damage. If I damaged her, it may well be the last thing I ever do."

Blade seemed satisfied with his sincerity. "So what now?"

"Now?" He looked at me. "We wait. The Hounds will not give up, they cannot be deterred, or made to abandon their hunt. Not by any of us. When they come, we slay them."

I took out my guns and got them ready. "How we gonna play this?"

"We can either let them breach or we can make an opening. I say opening, it will let us control where they come in."

I nodded at the wisdom. "Sounds good. So, any way to kill them that won't take half a clip?"

Donovan pursed his lips and thought. "Yes, actually." With that he reached to his side and pulled a sword out of his ass. "Use my blade."

An honest to god fae sword. I took it, held it, and admired it. It was an extension of my hand, my arm, my mind, such was the balance of this blade. Its blueish silver blade flashed in the light and I knew, knew this sword would not fail me. I also knew that what just happened was unusual.

"I will return her to you." I nodded at that. "And I am honored you trust me with her."

Donovan nodded. "In each our own way, we both love her. You honor me by letting my blade defend her."

With that, there was a sound and the lights flickered.

Our friends had tracked us down.

The wards flared on the west wall first. Made sense since we had come that way into the city. Next came the northern and southern walls, finally the eastern wards flared.

"Give them a moment, let the wards tire them." He nodded at me. "I'll be opening on the north side as its furthest from me and her."

I looked at Blade. "Stay back here with D man and the B." She nodded and got behind the two warriors.

"Be glad I understand flippantness is part of your nature cat."

I stared at the northern wall and waited. "Always D man, always."

The lights flickered again, and I could hear claws on the roof. Readying myself, I waited for the signal.

"Now." Came Donovan's warning.

The northern facing wall was where the kitchen was. I watched as the wall itself rippled as reality tried to tell the things that were attacking it that no, in fact you can't just walk through solid matter. Unfortunately, it lost that argument as the first pushed its way through. Much to my annoyance, a second and third came in at the same time before the wards went back up.

Three, with only myself and one other on the northern wall.

Sword in one hand, firearm in the other, I ran for the nearest monstrosity as I yelled at the elf to go after the furthest, and opened fire on the one in the middle.

I needn't have bothered. She had already slain that one and was on her way to the far one by the time I had loosed the last of the lead. I met my own in a single slice as it heedlessly tried to rush in. Three down, three slashes and four shots.

"Well done, Tyger." The green warrior said. "Your shots saved me time."

"It's Claw." I said as I readied for the next wave.

"Sear." She said with a grin. "Not my birth name, but one I earned."

The wards flickered again, four more got in. "Guess that makes you a fire brand."

She barked a laugh as she took two on at the same time. These hadn't run head long into our swords. They were being more cautious, smarter. I popped four more into one of mine, then turned to the other as the first fell. "Come on ugly, I need a new dance partner."

It lowered its head and made to lunge, but at the last moment stopped and lashed its whip like tendrils at me. Well, to be more precise at my gun hand. I didn't recognize the faint quick enough to stop it, but did manage to cut one of the little toothy maws free of the end of its skinny little neck. The one that I didn't slice knocked the gun from my now very numb hand.

Behind me I could hear my partner engaging with her own hounds, but I didn't dare risk a glance. Ugly started growling at me as it stayed just out of sword range. Keeping its eyes on me, it tried to circle to the left.

"Oh no ugly, I'm not falling for that." I had to give a little ground but I was not letting the thing circle past me. As I moved, I took a glance over to the other warrior. Both of hers were also keeping outside of sword range, but one had lost both of its little mouths and the other had lost the right one.

"I can't keep holding them, her wards are fighting me."

"Well," I tried a feint of my own and had the gratification of the damn dog falling for it. "We've killed five..."

I heard two more yelps. "Seven." Came from my left shoulder.

"That only leaves three. Just let them in."

"Done."

I turned and watched as first one came in, then the second, finally the third... then two more, then four more, then a huge one. Then behind the huge one, another five came.

Fuck.

"Furball, that is far more than the ten you alluded to."

Yeah, no shit. "I only saw ten in the alley, well... Eleven, but I had already killed one."

The other three warriors came and joined us. Blade called out behind me. "Why isn't she waking up?"

You know, at this point, that was a damn good question.

Chapter 20

Sweet Kisses

With what I could only guess was the pack leader here, our foes backed up, regrouped, and started to coordinate. The warrior and I fell back to her companions as well.

"That's a damn good question Donny boy, why isn't the Mistress of Chaos gracing us with her unique brand of cosmic horror?"

"I don't know, could it possibly be she hasn't slept in a week?" He snapped back.

"Shit." Betha had a different idea. "You kissed her on the forehead and told her to sleep well."

"You mean he enchanted her?"

"If I did that wasn't what I meant."

"You were annoyed she was so exhausted and wanted her rested."

"Of course I was annoyed." He said as he stood up. "Do you know how she's going to pout when she wakes and realizes I hadn't ridden her like a barmaid."

"I don't want to know." Blade said. "How do we wake her?"

Light flashed behind me and I looked back to see that Donnavan had donned his armor. He pulled his other sword from its scabbard and nodded. "How do you think?"

"Then kiss her damn it." Blade yelled.

The hounds had finally completely regrouped and were slowly advancing.

"Doesn't work that way." I said to Blade. "Donovan and I both love her, but neither of us are in love with her, not like that."

"She will sleep until rested."

"She will be well rested if she winds up dead." The punk bartender growled.

Betha sighed. "Shit." The word was more breath than word. I doubt the human heard it. I did, as did the other Sidhe. I glanced back just in time to see the armored warrior hop on the bed, straddle Sonja, whip off her helm and kiss her... deeply... like she was trying to lick her lungs.

Sonja's eyes snapped open just as the hounds started their attack.

The big one was definitely coordinating things, it stayed in the back, as seven swept from one side trying for a bee line to Blade, while the other's did the same. Donovan fell back to protect Blade, his girls fell back to protect him. I lashed out as I fell back as well. I had one trick that might work. It would work if they were, you know, normal dogs. But these were bad boys, not very good boys.

I took a deep breath and roared.

Funny thing about a tiger's roar. There is a subaudible component to it that will, for a moment, freeze even the bravest of the brave. It wasn't normally the kind of thing I would use in a group, but as it stood, we were all dead if I didn't. Behind me I knew the defenders were going to flinch, but the bulk of the sound wasn't aimed at them. I hoped it didn't just get us all killed.

The hounds didn't flinch, they froze.

Well, all but the big one.

It roared back in answer. Where mine was majestic, noble, and utterly terrifying, it sounded as if someone had thrown a bunch of nails into a blender and turned it on, while each of the nails was also scrapping across a black board, and Styrofoam was rubbing against Styrofoam.

In other words, it made my teeth wiggle and sweat.

That noise had one unforeseen side effect.

It pissed Mortis off.

One ton of pissed off shire came charging out of nowhere, it reared up and proceeded to bring its suddenly steel shod hooves straight down on the leader's head. For good measure the grey then kicked out and sent another one of the creatures to the great beyond.

With their momentum broken, the other warriors and I surged forward and began to battle the remaining hounds. As we did, the temperature in the room dropped drastically. The elves' armor was bright and shiny, the armor that charged up the middle making its way to its mount was anything but. Black, ghostly, cloying to the skin of its wearer, shadows, ichor, and pitch given metallic but still fluidic form.

She pulled a claymore from the horse's saddle and began to fight the hounds.

It was over in a matter of moments. Six sidhe, one cat, one barbarian, and a demented horse was more than enough to turn the tide, but not without injury.

I got hit twice more, three of the elves had to fall back with bleeding wounds, and Donovan was on the ground. In the end though, everyone was alive and safe. Or as safe as we could be.

Betha was getting her master out of his armor with shaking hands, begging him as she did. "Don't die, please, don't die on me."

He let out a weakened cough, the kind that has blood come up with it. "So, how long?"

"With luck many more years, my Master." She had the breast plate off, and his breathing was starting to ease. "You better not die on me, on us."

"No Sabetha." He captured her hands in his. "How long have you been in love with her?"

She closed her eyes and tears began to pour out. "Years my love. Years."

"Think you I would chastise you?"

"Should not you come first?"

"I remember not asking nor taking that from you."

Sonja came over, her shadow plate so much smoke in a high wind. "What did I miss?" She looked at me.

"A mage, they're not looking for the drugs, the mage sent the hounds, and apparently Sabetha is in love with you." At my words the silver sylvan's face turned crimson.

"I don't want to be sent away." She kissed Donovan's hand. "I love you."

"Yes, as I love her. But you are not in love with me, as I am not with her."

Blade too was starting to tear up. "Is he going to be getting rid of her now or something?"

"My love, you have no idea how proud I am of you." Donovan said as he sat up. "When you came to me, you were so hurt, so torn, I feared you no longer capable of love."

"Don't say that my lord." As she spoke the others came around taking off their helms and watching. They too started to cry. "I have always loved you."

Donovan nodded. "Aye, as only the broken can love a knight that has rescued them. But we both know, this is different."

"She'll not have me. How can she?"

Sonja spoke up. "Look not to interrupt, but I would prefer to speak for myself on that account."

Donovan laughed, so did his girls, finally Blade joined in. Laughing sidhe are contagious.

Chapter 21

Looking around at the aftermath, everything was a mess. Not just the bodies reality was rapidly rotting to get their offensive being out of this reality, but the interpersonal stuff too. I took Blade outside while the sidhe sorted themselves out.

"So, those are elves." The young woman was hugging herself as she spoke. Couldn't blame her, I would be too if this were my first rodeo. "So, no pointy ears?"

I shook my head. "I'm honestly not sure what the difference is, and I damn sure don't know the taxonomy, but no. No those aren't elves." I thought about it for a moment. "I mean, they are." I let out a sigh. "One of my best friend's daughters is like ¼ elf. Her grandmother is a full blood and doesn't get mad if you call her an elf. But I have also seen some of Donovan's girls get upset when called an elf. So, what the hell do I know?"

"Maybe it's like nationalities?"

"Could be." That actually made a weird kind of sense. "Or it could be that elf is a wholly human name for their people. Kind of like if you call a southern Athabascan an Apache they aren't likely to bother arguing."

"I thought an Apache was a helicopter."

"That too."

We both stared off into nothing for a few moments. "So that's what they look like."

I shrugged. "Or that's what our minds can handle." You never could be sure you were seeing the same thing others were when you dealt with shit like this.

"So how long before we have more of those dog things?"

"We shouldn't. Those tracked us, but by the time mage boy conjures up more of them, there won't be anything for him to scent to sic them on us. So, in other words, I'm not taking you back to that place." Of course, now he could track me if he saw me again too.

"So, what now?"

"Now? We'll look at what we know."

"I don't think we know a damn thing."

I shrugged. "We know the cartel didn't kill her. After all, had they, they wouldn't be looking for, well whatever the hell it was… is."

"They could have if she hid it before they got to her."

"That brings us to another point. She's dead, and so is the boy toy. Unless someone else was massacred in his apartment."

"In which case why are they still looking for the boyfriend?"

"Bingo."

"Isn't that spell or the herbs they are using, used to find money?"

"Value. Money can be anything of value." It not being money, money might be why they were having trouble finding it. "The point is the MacGuffin is something of value that at the very least one mage using demons is looking for, with the possibility of a second mage setting traps for you or rather her in your apartment then in his apartment."

"And we're no closer to finding out who actually killed Rayray."

The sound of a car door closing drew her and my attention. It was the mom again, only this time she had the man from the picture with her, the father. She looked pissed; he looked like he would have rather been heading off to the dentist.

"Well, if it isn't the regular." Blade said with her accent coming in thick. "Come clean to the missus?"

Abigail smiled at the two of us as she came up. "Something like that." They both stopped in front of me. "Claw, Blade, this is my husband, Mack."

I held out my hand much to his shock, but ingrained manners took over and he shook it anyway. Ah social brain washing. It didn't matter that I made him uncomfortable, it was simply what you did.

"My wife…" he looked over at Abigail. "She seems to think you can find out what actually happened… to our child."

"Well, that's a bloody start." Blade grumbled. "Ya daughter, you colossal wank, and you knew her."

"He never," He caught himself, "Never actually said it was… hell." He looked at his feet. "She kept ducking me, saying she didn't know me. There, happy?" He glared daggers at Blade.

"She's dead. No, I'm not happy. But in my presence, you'll give her some damn respect, or you'll have to have the cat pull me off your body."

He bowed up at the threat. His wife took his arm, and I stepped in front of Blade. "So, what changed your mind?"

He looked back at his wife, passed me to Blade, then back to me before deflating. "My son." I felt Blade move behind me. "The other one. He's, he's gotten involved with some people."

Abigail looked sickened. "Our son, well he just got a tattoo." She took a deep breath, as if the concept were so foreign to her as to border on blasphemy. "Two actually."

"What the hell is wrong with that?" Blade snapped before I could speak. In fairness it was a good question.

"It's what the tattoo is of, isn't it?" We all turned to see Sonja standing in the open doorway.

The mother nodded. "It's not his first. The first was an 88. We, we didn't think much about it. The next one was what he called a black sun, a pagan symbol he said." Tears started as she looked at Sonja. "His father and I, well, we didn't like it, but after losing one child."

"Pagan wasn't no contact." The father said. "We figured we could give him some space and he'd come around." At that he looked defeated. "We made him a deal. As long as he still came to church, he could believe anything he liked." Finally, the child in front of me morphed from a sniveling coward of a human, into a man as he accepted reality on its terms. "Last night, he came home, he and I had a couple of beers and he showed off his new 'ink'. It was a skull with an SS in it on his chest over his heart, and a swastika on his right arm." He nodded, horrified that this was the case. "Then he asked me to come with him to the next meeting. Said I believe all the things his buddies believe; the fall of western civilization, the great replacement, the fact that the queers at best needed re-education and if they couldn't be taught, they should be locked up so good decent people didn't have to see them."

I was stunned, and I wasn't the only one.

Sonja was unmoved. "And?"

Abigail spoke up. "That's not how we raised him." At those words, the father finished.

"Yes, it was." Holding his head high he looked at us. "I threw him out. I can't do anything for… for Rayzor. But I don't have to put up with that." He took a deep breath. "I failed my children. The least I can do is find out who murdered one of them."

Sonja nodded. "We'll find out. Until then, I suggest you and Blade speak, ask her about your daughter." She then nodded to me, and I followed her inside.

The sidhe were gone, and the look on her face let me know now was not the time to ask.

I don't like Nazis because, well, I grew up basically US army. The only thing worse than a commie was a Nazi. Sonja had her own feelings on them.

"Okay, what did I miss?"

I quickly gave her the run down. She cussed.

"That wasn't him in the apartment. Probably a roommate." She started pacing. "We need to find this guy before he winds up, well…" She made an off-hand gesture.

"Chunky salsa?" I asked.

She snorted. "Sometimes I love your humor." She nodded. "Yeah. We have to find the boyfriend. The mage you ran into didn't kill her, but the other one might have."

"You sure there are two?"

"Yeah. Hound boy didn't know she was dead, he also didn't know about the trap at the guy's apartment… if he did, he wouldn't still be looking for him. He'd assume the same as we did, that boyfriend was already out of the picture."

Good point. Not killed for the drugs, it was starting to look like she was killed for whatever lover boy stole. I looked back at Sonja and caught her in one of her thousand-yard stares. "What's up co-cheese?"

"I'm thick, I'm missing something… I just don't know what yet."

If she said she had missed something, then she did. But God if I knew what it was.

Chapter 22

Grady

We let the three of them into the house, and Sonja and I went to go see a cop about a body. We went down to Grady's home precinct and proceeded to make our way passed the desk and looked for the man. Much to my delight he was already at work, and sitting at his desk. It was early morning, so yeah, he was probably just getting in.

We made our way over, "What's shakin' bacon?"

He looked up at the two of us. "Dear god, why are you two here?"

"Got an id on the guy in the apartment?" Sonja asked.

He looked between us. "No, why?"

"Because we don't believe it was Derik Shields."

Grady made a face at that. "It's going to take some time, not only was the guy chunky salsa," A grin split my face at that one. "But parts of him were folded in upon themselves."

Ok, that was gross. "So, what are you doing?"

He rolled his eyes at us. "Typing up reports, you know, police work." He made a shooing gesture at the two of us and went back to his stack.

Well, we had found out what we needed to, Sonja and I started to head off when Grady said, "Wait." We both looked back. "Look, what makes you two think it's not him?"

I grinned. "Because last night I ran into a mage who thinks he's still alive, and thinks that the other bartender is the dead girl."

He blinked at us both, sighed, and took out a pad and grabbed a pen. "I'm going to regret this, but start from the beginning."

So, I laid out everything that had happened, how we got to that point, minus the hacker of course, and what had happened with the Dark Hounds, the Siege, and the Parents being at Sonja's place as we spoke. When I was done, he looked at me like I had grown another head.

"Dark Hounds?"

I nodded.

"Mages, plural, looking for, what did you call it, The Glazed MacGuffin?"

I nodded again.

He looked from me, to Sonja, to the phone on his desk. His mind was into some grand calculations, the kind of stuff that shaped entire orbits of life.

"Fuck it. I'm in." He grabbed his coat and his stuff, "Let's go talk to the family." We went outside and he got in his car, and followed us.

Chapter 23

The first place we went was back to Rayzor and Blade's apartment. Having a detective with us meant we weren't going to be in trouble for crossing the tape. I've never understood that on TV. Like the cops have already been there, yes. Sure, they weren't looking for what you are with your big idea's mister private dick, but here's the thing. They had already catalogued every print they could find. If they really wanted to, your new prints would be a cake walk to pick out. They would literally be the ones that weren't there before the tape got taken down.

So, we got Grady to go in first, and all of us put on blue gloves.

Once we were inside, he asked. "Ok so," He looked around. "What did we miss?"

Sonja started scanning the room, meanwhile I started picking over the debris. The couch looked as if it had been crumpled up like a ball of paper, and I knew from previous experiencing some of the 3d object was poking through to 4d space. At least I hoped it was just 4d. The higher up you go on that number before the d the weirder things got.

"Well," Sonja began, "We know for a fact that Rayzor is looking into things herself."

That got Grady's attention, "The victim is looking into their own murder?"

"In a way." She said.

"But... wouldn't she know who did it?"

It was a good question... why had I never asked it? I stopped what I was doing to hear what Sonja said next.

"You're mistaking meat for spirit. The meat was there at the moment of death as was the spirit. But while the meat may or may not know what happened, it's traumatic as hell. That means the spirit hadn't had time to deal with and internalize what happened. She's pissed, she's hurt, and she is confused. She may not even know she's dead." Sonja sighed. "But given she pushed Blade out of the way of harm, I'm willing to bet she's well aware of her death."

He nodded. "Ok, so she likely knows she's dead, but not how? Am I understanding that correctly?"

"Ever been in a car accident?"

"Yeah."

"The first few seconds after it, did you know what had happened?"

I thought about the ones I had been in myself.

Bam! You're rattled, you know you got hit, you know you're hurt, but you don't know where, or what to start with. I was completely rattled more than a few times.

"Yeah, you're in shock." Grady said.

"Bingo." Sonja cocked her head over to the side and narrowed her eyes. "Most spirits are when they first cross. It's why some have no idea what's happening. A lot of them go on with their idea of what their life was and never know anything happened."

"Ok, but this one you think does." He and I both watched as she walked over to the bookshelf.

The shelf itself had been emptied during the search, either during the ransacking or the investigation. Sonja moved the bookshelf and picked up one of the anime collectibles that had been knocked over. A flash drive fell to the floor, and she bent down to pick it up. "She pushed Blade back out to the hall, and she was, well... she was all cut up and bloody."

Grady blinked. "But she was shot, beaten."

I knew this one! "Sonja sees the world differently from you or I. She sees you, the real you. All the wounds, all the pain, all the pieces of ourselves we've cut off or ignored. To her they are bright bloody wounds on all of us."

She was holding up the USB. "It's new, and the writing on it is Spanish." Grady came over and Sonja handed it to him. "Looks like our girl made it home from Mexico after all."

The flash drive wasn't your basic black, it was a bright red with a palm tree on it. Under that were the words, Bienvenida al Paraíso. My eyes went big. "Is this what the mages are looking for?"

Sonja shrugged.

"Why didn't my people find this? Or the people who ransacked this place before you got here?"

Sonja let out a sigh, "Well," she gestured to the book self. "The dust on the shelf lets you know nothing's been moved in a while before everything was pushed off. But the base of the giant robot was clean. Given what it is, or I should say who it is, this collectable has a hidden space inside it. I used to have this robot in disguise." Sonja shrugged, "What? I'm a nerd." She shrugged. "If I had to guess," she started rearranging the toy. "This was actually stored in its other form." She finished the transformation and held it up to show the dust. "Voila."

Grady grinned. "A hiding place where only someone familiar with either the toy or this home would have found it."

"I wonder what's on it." I craned my neck as if changing the position of my head would give me some clue.

"One way to find out." Grady went over to his bag and took out a laptop. He set it up and went to plug the thing in, when I stopped him.

"Hold on there a minute chief. What if that's a kill drive?"

He looked at me and raised an eyebrow. "A what?"

I looked at him. "A flash drive that either has a virus, malware, or worse, it's secretly a load of capacitors and as soon as you plug it in it will pop your computer with a built-in charge."

Grady looked at the thing in his hands as if it were going to blow up now. "Thanks." Then he shook his head. "Let's give this to one of the tech guys." He looked at Sonja. "Ok, we now know she came home before she died. So where are her bags?"

Interesting question. "So, she takes boy toy, heads down to Mexico, has a vacation, her and boy toy pick this up, likely as a souvenir, and come home." I looked around. "They get back to New York, she comes here first, then goes back out and gets killed before she can deliver the goods." I started pacing around. "How did she get home?"

"How did she get back from Mexico?" She looked over at Grady.

"We've already looked for her at the airport, but we haven't seen her yet." He then cocked his head. "But... she wasn't exactly a high priority."

The best of the cops are overworked and underpaid. Worse, they are asked to do far too much. Most cops are asked to handle shit they have no business handling. So, even the good ones are asked to do shit they aren't trained for. Then of course you got the bad ones.

Sonja looked over at him. "Yeah, what's one more dead trany, right?" She squared herself against his onslaught, "Worse, she was a mule. I mean, we're all better off now that she's dead."

Grady grew red hot; his anger was easy to see. I waited for the normal programmed reaction to this kind of challenge. It's a hard job, it's dangerous, we're the thin blue line, be grateful commoner, comply or die. All of it played out on his face.

"We..." He stopped himself. "It happens. That don't make it right, but it does." He deflated. "We do, we do what we can. I mean, if we aren't seen closing cases, doing something, then... It's bullshit." He nodded to himself. "It's all excuses. I wrote her off." He looked Sonja in the eyes. "And if it wasn't for your meddling..." He left the rest unsaid.

Sonja merely nodded. "Do better."

He took a deep breath. "So, she's hurt, she wants revenge, and she can push things. As she goes, how long before she puts together what happened to her?"

Sonja had started looking around at the mess again. "It depends. Right now, she's experiencing everything at a different rate than she's used to. Think of it like suddenly being submerged in molasses. Everything is slower. Then, when something important happens, everything speeds up like someone hit fast-forward."

I walked into the kitchen. It could be seen from the door, and it too had been ransacked.

"The spirit mind experiences the world in a more dream-like state. It's why most spirits can't touch real things. It's the same reason you can't touch or really do stuff while you're dreaming. But once a spirit can, it's lucid dream time for them."

Containers for sugar, salt, coffee, flour, and other stuff were on the floor, all opened. Each thing had a number tag by it and doubtlessly had been photographed. I looked from the floor, to the counter, back to the floor.

"So you're saying she can control things like someone can in a dream?"

"If coffee on floor, and coffee on floor only half the container... Why coffee bag on counter opened but not poured in?" I asked.

Both of them stopped and looked at me.

"What?" Grady asked.

I pointed to the knocked over half empty bag of coffee that had been marked, numbered, and photographed, that was on the counter, and the cylinder container on the floor that was spilled but could obviously hold more coffee. It too had been photographed.

Grady came over and picked up the bag. He opened it and poured it out. There, amongst the grounds was a key.

"Son of a bitch." The cop said.

Chapter 24

Back down at the station Grady took us to the guy whose job it is to catalogue everything. Now contrary to popular belief, there is more than one person working in evidence. What isn't exaggerated is these poor guys and gals are left cataloging everything. Every time some flat foot mislabels something, it's their thankless job to figure that out. I don't know what it's like in other realities, but the men and women of the NYCPO's Department of Evidence have seen it all, literally.

If anyone knew what that key was for, it would be them.

"I don't know what to tell you. These things are a dime a dozen and mass produced. The housing authority uses them for their lockers, the transit authority uses them for their lockers, O'Hair, JFK, Greyhound, hell half the transit points on the eastern seaboard use these, Maine to Jersey."

Great so much for that. "And the flash drive?" I asked.

"Smart thing not putting it on the laptop. First off, it's not a popper, that's the good news. The bad is there are three files on it. Two are full of vacation pictures. The third is corrupt, it's huge, or reporting as huge at any rate, but it won't open."

Sonja raised an eyebrow. "What kind of file is it?"

"Oh, it's a data file. Probably someone's attempt at coding. When I open it up, it's just gibberish." He turned and pulled the flash drive out of the computer's USB port. "Tried to run a decryption algorithm, but nada." He handed it back to Grady. "I don't think it's part of your case."

"Why is that?" Grady asked.

The tech smiled. "Well, unless your case was from the 90's, those pictures aren't relevant. They look like they were part of a new year's celebration. Probably originally taken on a film camera and transferred over to digital."

Grady nodded. "Thanks. Um, is there any way to figure out where the key came from?" The tech looked at him funny. "Figured I would ask."

"That probably is part of your case. But for the life of me I have no way of telling you where it is to."

He nodded. "Thanks Jeff."

"No problem, man."

The three of us walked out of evidence with Grady looking ready to chew nails. Once outside he asked, "So what now?"

I shrugged.

Sonja, however, got that look on her face. What look? The look that said a synapse has fired. "Let's go talk to mister rapist. He still in the hospital?"

Grady nodded. "Yeah, he had a heart attack and is under guard."

"Well alright, alright, alright." I said. "Let's go talk to a prick."

***

At the hospital we cruised our way to the door that had two armed patrolmen standing in front of it. Both of them nodded to Grady as we went by them and into the room. It wasn't the room the guy had been in yesterday. Was it yesterday? No, I think it was the day before. Doesn't matter they moved him and he didn't look good. Upon seeing Sonja his pale pallor did the impossible and went even whiter.

I grinned at him, "Hello Motto." His eyes darted to me, then to the cop. "We gots questions for you."

He looked at Grady. "Get them out of here."

I grinned wider. "Play nice and we'll be gone fast."

He didn't bother looking at me. Anger gave him some of his former color back. "Get them out of here or I ain't talking. That lawyer you people gave me said not to answer any more questions for you unless she was here."

Grady made a face. "He's right." He let out a sigh. "I should call his lawyer."

Sonja looked at him. "Did she look you in the eyes as she squeezed your heart? Did she say she would be back?" Her words were dreamy, as if she were sleeping.

Richard "Ricky" Potts grew so pale he might have been having a second heart attack right then and there. His eyes went wide, and the monitors showed that yes, for a second his heart did indeed stop. Sonja waved a hand and the rhythm equalized once more.

"Oh no, you're not going anywhere. But I'll tell you what. If you corporate with me, then I can put her to rest before she gets enough power to come back and do it right."

His breathing was rapid, his eyes were wide, but he nodded.

"Now, you told these nice people that the guys who took you, who beat you, who were at the motel, that they were after you because of the drugs."

Ricky nodded again, still not speaking.

"Only they aren't after the drugs Mr. Potts. When they went after Blade and Claw, the guy said he wasn't after the drugs."

"I swear," He looked at me, at Grady, at the wall, anywhere but at Sonja. "They were looking for the drugs."

"Did they say that, or did you assume that?" I asked. I mean it was a fair question.

"What else would they be looking for?"

Bingo.

Sonja smiled now. Look, I'm a big-toothed predator. The human mind sees me grin, it brings up feelings. It why I've learned a few different ways of smiling. Sonja was like that too. Most of the time she had this little lop-sided grin that said she was amused. Sometimes she had this smile that said she was mildly embarrassed, that one usually when someone gives her a compliment. But sometimes she had this smile. It promised pain, torture, heartache, misery. She smiled and you could see hell itself grinning at you.

Hell had now found Mr. Richard Potts.

Poor Grady had never been this close to hell before, I felt for him. I remember my first time.

"What did they say they were looking for Richard? What were they asking about?"

"The key, they were asking me where the key was. I don't know. I swear. I don't know what key they were talking about. I thought it was wherever the drugs were hidden."

"Rest now."

With that, our little piggy went to sleep.

The three of us made our way out of the room, Grady looked almost as shaken as the man in the bed.

"Is, is he going to be, ok?"

Sonja shook her head. "Not unless we can put Rayzor to bed before she can finish the job."

"Why hasn't she done so already?"

"Because it takes a lot of anger, a lot of hate to do that. She's not there yet."

As we made our way back to the joys of the city, Grady looked back. "I'm surprised you're trying to save him to be honest,"

"I'm not. I'm trying to save her."

Grady just nodded. "Well, we have the key, now what?"

"Humans are creatures of habit. It makes you guys predictable." I said. "That key goes to some place where I am betting, she felt the contents would be safe."

He nodded. "Make sense. So, what, can we ask her?"

Sonja shook her head. "No, we go to Blade. Seeing the key will just make her more hurt, angrier. It will complete her transformation that much faster."

I knew as soon as she said that, that Grady would ask. "Transform into what?"

"A Wraith."

Chapter 25

A Trip to the Keys

Back at the Warehouse, Blade was a little confused to see the good detective. "What's this wanker doing here?" were her exact words. We explained that the good detective was now wholly committed to the cause of helping to find the killer. We told her about what we found in the apartment.

"So, Rayray stashed a key in some coffee and the flash drive in one of the collectibles?" She seemed to be seriously thinking it over. "What kind of coffee?"

Grady raised an eyebrow, "Does it matter?"

"Oy it matters. She drank her stuff, I drank mine. If it was in my coffee, then I was meant to find the key then, wasn't I? If it was hers then she was coming back for it." God, I love this girl. Great brain on her.

"Um, it was decaf, a Larder House breakfast blend." I said.

Blade blinked. "Decaf, you sure?"

"Yes, why?"

"We're bartenders, we don't drink decaf." She seemed to think about that for a moment as she walked around. "Neither her nor I kept that stuff in the house."

Interesting, "How about Larder House?"

"Now that's normal. We always get our coffee from them, its right next to our gym."

Grady's head went up "That Gym got lockers?"

***

Freebooter Gym was a standalone, not part of any chain, and catered to a group of people who may not feel comfortable elsewhere. As a place that catered to the so-called Alphabet Mafia, it had pride flags everywhere. Blade went in first, followed by me and Sonja. No one so much as glanced up. When Grady came through the door, you'd have sworn it was an old western. Slowly, starting at the front, people stopped what they were doing and looked our way.

Blade held out her hand. "Give me the key, I'll check her locker."

Grady groused. "I should really go with you."

Sonja leaned into him and whispered, "You got a warrant?"

The girl who had been working the counter had made her way over to us. "May I help you officer?"

Blade gave her a smile. "He's with me." The woman raised an eyebrow at that. Blade's face fell. "Ray's gone."

The woman turned and looked at her. "What? What happened?"

"Someone, look, she was killed, its why the cop's here."

The woman was horrified. "Oh my god, what happened?"

Grady stepped up, "That's what we're trying to figure out." He might as well have farted in church and bragged about it.

"Relax Becca," A familiar woman said as she came up. She had been deadlifting before she noticed us come in. "If he's with those two he can't be all bad."

I grinned as Red walked up. "Hi-a toots." We hugged. It was nice to be hugged by someone taller and more athletic than I was. Red was a local power lifter and friend of the family, Kyle's family. At well over 6 foot and she was cut like a diamond, I was happy to see her and her red brush cut. "So, this is where you spend your time huh?"

"It's a good place. So, who's the cop?"

Thankfully, Grady had enough sense not to try to introduce himself.

"He's the detective working the case." I looked back at the guy. "Is it possible he could go with Blade to look at the locker? I mean, we are looking for evidence."

The desk jockey looked at Red who nodded. She then smiled at Blade and Grady. "Of course, right this way." The three of them went off, and once out of ear shot Red asked.

"So, what's going on?"

Sonja shook her head. "Dead Trans Woman, grieving mom, restless ghost, blackmail, the cartel, at least two different mages, and a whole lot of shit."

Red looked at the both of us, "And Amanda's woowoo squad isn't all over it?"

I shrugged, "No clue. They had written her off as a drug mule on account of the balloon she had in her at time of death. So maybe it hasn't hit her desk."

Red nodded. "Maybe."

Sonja cocked her head "Did you know the two of them?"

She looked over her shoulder at where Blade and the Cop had gone. "No. Not really. I mean I had seen the twins around, but that's it." She looked lost for a moment. "Was it a hate crime or just a matter of someone taking out a business rival?"

"Don't know, heard anything?"

"Not really. But I'm just an enforcer. It's Snake you'd want to talk to."

Sonja lowered her voice, "Can you arrange it?"

Red shook her head. "Not as long as you got the tag along. But I can tell him you want to talk."

"Thanks."

"No problem. So, is he a good guy?"

"He went from punching the clock to actually wanting to figure it out, so…"

She grunted. "So, an improvement." She looked to where the three of them were coming back. "I'll message him. Hell, he might be in a mood." With that she went off.

The woman peeled off as Blade and Grady made their way back to us with a large gym bag. "We're good to go."

"What's inside it?" I asked.

"Her travel stuff. Three bathing suits, all smelling of cocoa butter, couple of pairs of jeans and two long shirts." Blade then held up a matching flash drive, "And this."

We turned and made our way out of the building and onto the street, when the whole damn area went dark as if someone had turned off the lights. Daylight to darkness is not a good sign. My ears pricked as I heard what sounded like someone running straight for us. As I turned to intercept them, I heard Blade grunt and go "Hey."

As suddenly as the lights went out, they came back, and there in the distance, running hells to leather, was a guy with the gym bag.

Word of wisdom. Don't run from a cat, it's not smart.

I hit all fours and was after him before anyone else could even move. My clothing is in fact tailored for this, so it wasn't a big deal, but my shoes flew off my hind paws. Still haven't managed to find a good design when it comes to them.

Dude bro thought he was in the Olympics the way he was running, then he looked back. His hind brain took one look at me and decided he wasn't fast enough. He started running faster.

Now we're getting somewhere.

I almost had him when he made my day. With a fluid move that let me know he wasn't new to this, he went to free running.

"Parkor!" I said as I bounced off the car ahead of me to change directions.

He went down an alley, over a dumpster, then up a wall at the end and over to the next alley.

I went over the dumpster then over the wall.

He rolled when he landed and was on his feet moving again.

I landed on my paws and kept going.

He hit the street and hung a 90 thanks to a lamp post.

I bounced off the area ahead of him.

He lost his footing and skidded onto his back side trying to find purchase with his hands and feet.

I pounced.

He screamed.

People around us were giving me a wide berth, and I couldn't blame them. I also couldn't reassure them I wasn't going to actually eat him... not given the fact that I had my mouth around his upper arm.

The good news was he wasn't struggling.

The bad news was he was still screaming.

Please, understand this. I had trained for this my whole life. Catching men like this was not only part of my training, it was why I was engineered. This was second nature. So was the urge to shake. It wouldn't kill him, I didn't have anything vital. But if I shook, he would be going to the hospital.

I looked at my hands and realized my claws were out. I needed options that didn't keep triggering me.

When in doubt, smart ass. It's how I had gotten control of myself my whole life, how I broke the conditioning they tried to instill in me from birth.

I let go of his arm, swept his legs when he tried to get up, and then sat on him. Mister I'm going to steal the bag now had a mouth full of cat butt. He was lucky I was wearing pants or things would have been quite intimate.

Things went dark again, and my 'friend' tried to get out from under me.

"Stop that, or you're gonna set me off again. You want to be tiger chow?"

He stopped wiggling and the light came back. Little fucker was powered. "Good boy, now stay put and let the nice cop come and collect you, or I will chase you again." With that I got off him and waited.

As soon as I was off him, I realized who it was. "Hi Derik, we've been looking for you."

Derick didn't move, didn't twitch, didn't speak.

Smart boy.

Chapter 26

Back at the precinct, Derik was cooling his heels in an interrogation room. Grady meanwhile was in with his captain trying to explain why he needed two civilians in there with him while he talked to the guy. The three of us sat and watched the play of shadow figures that showed though the blinds.

I leaned over to Sonja, "Think we should tell the captain we know Kyle?"

Sonja leaned over towards me, "You want to get the guy fired?"

"Who's Kyle?" Blade asked in the same conspiratorial whisper.

"Kyle Savage." I told her.

Her eyes went wide. "The Savage? Mister 'I took a shotgun to the chest' Kyle Savage?" I nodded. "Bloody hell."

"Yep."

"So why would it get Grady fired?"

Sonja chuckled. "Because most Captains don't like Kyle. He tends to go against the cop bro code, but no one can do anything to him because it would be a PR nightmare."

Yeah, Kyle didn't buy the thin blue line shit. He turned on bad cops, held those in his house to the protect and serve standard, and his house loved him for it. Why? Because he put his body on the line. Among the rank and file, he was both the standard rookies held themselves to as well as the one who was there. For those that just wanted to go home at night, he was bad news. How? Everything he did made them look bad. Because of that, there was a small cult of cops that idolized him. It also didn't help that he was a bit of a media darling, what with his twin brother being a Broadway actor turned Veterinarian and the fact that both brothers used their wealth to help out several charities.

New York loved Kyle Savage.

"So, what? You mention Savage's name and they fire the guy?"

"More like he suddenly finds himself on the shit list." I said. "He starts pulling bullshit duties, gets crap cases, and put in a position where he's not closing. Then when he's up to his neck in orchestrated failure, they offer him a quiet, early retirement."

Sonja shrugged, "It's not like the captain doesn't know who we are. I mean you kind of stick out."

"Yes, but we're not pulling on his rep. We don't do that, and we're golden."

Blade nodded. "In other words, you don't name drop, and the captain in there treats you two like you're regular people."

I nodded. "That's the hope."

The door opened and said captain's face made an appearance. "You two, in here, now."

I suddenly had flashbacks to training and my CO.

We both came in with Blade right behind us.

"Oh no, she stays outside."

Blade held up her hands and went back to sit down.

Once the two of us were inside, the captain slammed the door. She was an older woman, probably looking down the barrel of retirement. Black hair and dark eyes, it was simple to tell she wasn't thrilled with us.

"Give me one good reason why I shouldn't have you two brought up on charges?"

I quickly went through everything that had happened in the last few days. Then all the stuff that the police could prove. "For what?"

"Interfering in an investigation."

Uh, wrong thing to say.

"Which investigation would that be? The one into the dead mule?" Sonja looked over at Grady. "Or maybe the one where the cartel is in town and the black mailer and rapist?" As Sonja spoke, the woman's eyes narrowed. "Or maybe it's some other investigation. One I'm unaware of, one we haven't been throwing every relevant detail over to you?"

She sat down and looked at the three of us. "I'll have you know, that I gave Detective Grady here the murder of that girl because he wasn't needed for the Synagogue case." She looked over at Grady, "I was unaware that it had just been written off."

Grady had the grace to look at his shoes before he spoke. "Captain, with…"

"Shut it Nate." She looked at the man. "I, like you, figured it was an open and shut case. Unlike you, I figured it would actually be worked and you would at least find out the woman's name."

His chin went up, "I did!"

"No, you found out who she was when she was a kid and that was based on a youth program that we ran in the 00s. These two found out who she was, where she was living, and what happened to her."

At that, he looked up. "Early retirement?" She nodded. "Damn."

"Nate, you been going through the motions for the last two years. I don't need a half ass. These two just saved your bacon." She looked back at us. "The case you two interfered with was whether or not Detective Grady got to keep his job." She nodded at us. "Now, now, he's your responsibility 'til this is over." She looked back at Grady, "Then you will need to have a nice long think about whether or not you want an early pension."

With that, we were out of the office. I looked over at Grady. As dressing downs went, that should have been private. The problem was, had it been, we wouldn't have also got chastised. I patted the poor guy on the shoulder.

"Nate huh?"

He nodded. "Nathaniel actually."

Sonja looked at him. "Let's go take care of this, and then you can contemplate your future."

He went to nod, then stopped. "You know what? No, fuck it. I got tired because of the grind. Thankless job, thankless people, and I never felt like I made a damn difference." He turned and looked at us, "So let's go make one."

"Damn straight." I said.

So, there we were, locked in a room with a man who had made the mistake of trying to run from me. He was obviously reliving that chase as soon as I walked in. I went to one corner,

Sonja went to the other, and Grady sat down in the chair opposite of the guy.

"I want a lawyer."

"Smart guy." Grady got back up. "I'll go get you one." He looked at me and asked. "You guys keep him company, will you?"

Bingo. His eyes went wide. "I ain't saying nothing to no cop without a lawyer."

"No, no, I got that. I'll go get you one." Grady stuck his head out of the door. "Can we get the public defender in here?" He looked back at the guy. "I can go out and get one, or I can stay here with you. Which is it?"

He crossed his arms but kept looking my way.

"Fair enough. Well since you're not going to talk, you mind if we do?" He gestured to Sonja and me. "Good." He sat back down and turned the chair almost completely always from the guy. "So, the mages, you guys really think there are two of them?"

Sonja nodded. "Definitely. One of them is making those spells that calls forth the tentacular monstrosity, like the one in Blade and Rayray's place. The other one is using Dark Hounds."

"Wait, Dark Hounds?"

The little fucker knew what those were.

Grady ignored him and pressed on. "Which one was the cartel?"

"The Dark Hounds." I said. "They are also the ones with the spell that's looking for money."

Sonja disagreed. "Na, that's got to be the second group. That one is the one that went to the apartments."

I nodded. "That's right, the ones looking for the money are the ones that do the hentai."

"Now wait a damn minute."

"You know, technically other than the fact that someone died in his apartment, we got nothing to hold this guy on. His PD will have him out of here in, what do you think? An hour?"

"Well, he did try to steal that bag from Blade." I said.

But the cop shook his head. "No, I didn't see that. It was dark. All I saw was him run and then you running after him. All circumstantial." He turned back to the guy. "Sorry Mister Shields. You're absolutely correct. You know what? Since Claw here isn't a cop, would you like to press charges against her for tackling you?"

Derik Shields looked between us and spoke. "Look, you got to protect me."

"Now why would we do that? Do you know something about a case I am working on?"

He looked back and forth between us. "You're really not going to charge me?"

"I don't know Mr. Shields, have you committed a crime?" He stayed silent. "If you haven't committed a crime, and you don't have any information on our case, then..." Grady spread his hands. "Then you're free to go with my apologies."

With that Grady sat back and smiled.

Meanwhile Derik Shields sat there and sweated.

The door opened and a beleaguered man poked his head in. "You better not have been asking my client any questions without his representation." His voice was forceful, but it was obvious he had said this so many times that he had been ground down by the system.

"Actually Dave. This young man is free to go."

Dave, the public defender looked at the cop, then his client. "You're not charging him or holding him on anything?"

"Nope. Hell, he might want to press charges against ol' Claw here. She's the one who caught him after a mugging that I can't confirm he was responsible for. Yes he ran, yes she chased, but come on. We both know you could get that thrown out in what? Ten minutes?"

"And you haven't asked him any questions."

"Well, that's not quite true. I did in fact ask him if he had committed any crimes, or if he had information on a case I'm working."

"Does he?"

"I don't know. How about we leave you alone with your client for a few moments, and I'll get started on his release paperwork." With that, all of us started for the door.

"Wait." Said Derik. We all stopped. "Can, can I talk to the lawyer for a few moments before I answer your questions?"

Grady smiled. "Of course." He nodded to David. "We'll be right outside."

Chapter 27

Pay the Ferryman

Twenty minutes, two coffees, and a bag of chips later Grady, Sonja, and I were back in the room, in our positions, and staring at the pipsqueak and his lawyer. Derik was fidgeting while his lawyer looked tired. He met eyes with the detective and gave him a look that said it all. He was not being paid enough for this bullshit.

"Before we begin, my client admits to no wrong doing or crime. What he was doing was participating in an impromptu vacation with his girlfriend. As part of that he met up with a friend and colleague to participate in a rite that his group must complete at least once in their life. I believe you will find that is covered under religious liberty."

Grady pursed his lips. "Ok, I'll bite. Start at the beginning."

Derik hung his head, avoiding everyone's gaze. "So, Raigan calls..."

"The girl?" Grady clarified.

"Yeah, so she calls me up and says she's going to have to cancel one of our… dates. You have to understand what a fascinating creature she is, or was. Being with her, well… I'm not gay. I mean yeah she was a man, but she was a woman? Like my masculinity was so much greater than hers, that she was my woman."

In a cold voice Sonja said, "Get on with it."

"Anyway, she said she was headed down to Mexico to this resort. That she had won it but had to go now due to reasons, and well… I asked if she needed a plus one." Derik took a deep breath. "She said yes, and well. We went. Things were great but she said she needed to go do something alone, and I was like good because, well, I did too. See I had a buddy down there that I needed to see. A higher-ranking member of my order, so really this was perfect."

"What order?" Grady asked.

"The Knights of the Void."

Sonja actually growled. Like she did me proud growled.

Grady looked over to her. "I take it you're familiar with them?"

"Children playing with elder gods."

Derik's chin went up, "I'll have you know that I am a High Fein of the Sixth Ring." Either he realized how silly that sounded or he understood the look Sonja was giving him. "Anyway. I went and met with Carlos, he's a Reverend Father, and I went through my anointment."

Grady looked at him, bored. "So far, my panties ain't wet. Get to the good stuff or I'll kick your ass out of here."

The little cult boy swallowed hard and nodded. "When I was getting dressed, I noticed that I had dropped the USB that I had bought and used to store the, um, video, that I had... anyway I picked it up and left." He sighed. "Only when I got back to the room, the USB drive was still plugged into my laptop."

"What was on the USB drive?" Grady asked.

"Couple of pictures, nothing big, not until I saw the data file."

Grady shrugged, "What about it? It's gibberish." But Derik shook his head.

"No, it's, it's encrypted. Unless you have the file meant to read it." He took a deep breath. "It's block chain."

That got my attention. "Crypto? How much?"

He looked at the wall. "It's Moneda De La Muerte... and it's got three hundred thousand coins."

The lawyer was looking at his client as if he had grown a second head.

"At what point did you realize what it was?"

Sonja spoke up, "These idiots all use the coin of death, it's how they trade the shit they deal in back and forth without getting caught. He knew what it was as soon as he plugged it in."

"So, you stole from your High Priest?"

"If it's found it's ours." He looked over at Sonja, "Tell them."

"When it comes down to it, they're magical scavengers. If he hadn't taken it, his Priest would have probably drummed him out of their little club."

Grady looked at him, "So what went wrong?"

Derik shook his head. "I have no idea. Raigan got back, and said we had to go now. That we were going to fly into Jersey and take a bus back home. She was scared. So I figured someone had found her package. Once I got home, Carlos had called me, he wanted the drive back. He was panicked. I thought it was a test, so I told him it was mine now. That's when he said he would get it back. I haven't been home since. Then I found out about Tod, and what happened at my apartment. When I went to look for the drive, I, I didn't know where it was, I couldn't find it. Raigan came back and started throwing things into bags, I figured she had picked it up."

Wow, I shook my head "Damn dude, you're fucked."

Grady seemed to be digesting the information.

Sonja said one word.

"Bullshit."

Chapter 28

Grady and I both looked over to the corner where Sonja was propped up, arms crossed, glaring daggers at the guy. "Bullshit." She said again. Derik fidgeted in his seat and the lawyer had the dawning realization that he was not in fact getting out of here as quickly as he hoped.

"What do you mean, bullshit?"

"I mean this guy just sat here and lied to our faces. His entire story is bullshit."

Derik sat there definitely.

"Normally, I would ask follow up questions, try to find the hole in the story." The detective said. "Inconsistencies and things like that. After all, we don't want this to turn into a he said she said situation." Derik actually begin to have a smug look on his face. "Do you have anything to back up your assumption Ms. Dee?" Everyone looked over to the red head in the corner.

"First off, we know that Mr. Potts was unaware of Rayzor but became aware and blackmailed her into being a mule." Derik sat still; Grady had raised an eyebrow. "As part of the smuggles drugs into the country, she was sent to a resort in Mexico. Now why would they let her go by herself or let anyone other than

Mr. Potts go with her?" Derik paled. "The only way Shields would be on this trip would be if he was the leash to the mule. But why would Mr. Potts suddenly come back into Rayzor's life and know that Rayzor was vulnerable to manipulation? After all, she managed to bamboozle her own father for a while. No, someone had to tell Mr. Potts who Rayzor was, and that same person would then be culpable enough that he too could be the lead to the mule."

The more she spoke the paler Derik Shields became. "Now wait just a damn moment."

"When they got down to Mexico, they did the tourist thing including to buying kitsch. The problem is, had it just been a flash drive that was laying around as Derik said, it wouldn't have old pictures on it, they would be new." Derik wasn't looking at anyone anymore and was all but vibrating out of his seat. "I have no doubt there is a Carlos, but I doubt he's a high priest. I think while Rayzor was being given her package and what was undoubtably a harrowing experience for her, you or your accomplice made a copy of the files, all the files that were there. After all you only had so much time." She cocked her head and continued. "You also would have had to disable the access of the original files. I'm guessing you wiped the PC in some way. The reason that the guys downstairs thought the file was corrupted instead of recognizing a block chain is because you split the file, half on one drive, half on the other."

The lawyer shook his head. "Do you have any proof of any of this?"

Sonja surprised me and nodded. "Once his computer is finished being gone through, I am sure you will find the link between Mr. Sheilds and Mr. Potts, but more importantly, if what he said was true, Rayzor wouldn't have bothered to hide the drives or the key. She wouldn't have known they were important. My guess is he bragged about it on the plane thinking her too weak to do anything about it." She then looked dead into Derik's soul, "Did she get it off of you when you insisted on joining the mile high club?"

With an explosion of energy, Derik was out of the chair and moving over to Sonja. I don't know what he thought he was doing, but whatever it was changed when his chin ran face first into her foot.

There, on the floor, was Derik Sheilds.

His lawyer looked up, "I believe my client was provoked by Ms. Dee's wild accusations."

Grady nodded. "Of course. We'll get him a doctor in here and send him on his way with our apologies. I would offer to charge Ms. Dee with assault, but as she hasn't really moved, I think it may be hard to prove." Grady got up, "We're going to leave you two alone now. I suggest your client decides to amend his bullshit story, or we're going to cut him loose."

With that the three of us were out of the interrogation room and Grady looked ready to chew nails. "What the hell was that?"

"Do you think I'm wrong?"

"No, no I don't. But he might skate now without giving us anything to work with."

I shook my head. "He won't. Whoever his partner is, the guy's obviously turned against him. Between him and the Cartel, this is the safest place he can be, especially since we have both drives."

Grady ran his hand through his hair. "So, what's the play?"

Sonja shrugged. "Get him a doctor and let's go see what's on that other drive. If I'm correct, we'll know, if I'm wrong, we'll know."

Grady called for a medic and gave orders to move Derik to holding until he said otherwise. Then we went down to evidence to see if we could confirm the information.

Once downstairs Grady handed over the drive, and told the tech what we thought it was.

While we waited for the tech to do his wizardry, Grady looked back and forth between the two of us. "Look, I'm not saying you're right or wrong," He looked over his shoulder, "We'll know some of that in a moment. But you were obviously close to the mark to set him off like that."

I went to agree with the cop, until I looked up and saw Sonja's thinky face. "I missed something."

"What do you mean?" Getting her to say things out loud was a good way to get that supercomputer to go slow enough for us mere mortals to keep up with it.

Sonja started pacing, "It's, he…" She began to chew on her bottom lip.

"Sonja, talk to us."

"His response was too violent. What's more he would need a way to get out with one of if not both drives, and he wouldn't do that by attacking us." As she paced, her mind wasn't here. Where it was, I couldn't tell you. "It was mentioning that the drives were meant to be used together that set him off." She stopped moving. "One drive, no problem. Both drives, but not knowing it was a binary problem, no problem. Knowing the drives were part of a binary problem..." Her eyes went wide.

Three things happened all at once.

One, Sonja turned and tried to make her way to the computer in a big hurry.

Two the tech said "Holy fuck."

Three, the lights went out.

The fourth came a few breaths later; screaming.

Chapter 29

Darker and Dumber

The darkness was just as unnatural as it had been on the street. Given the fact that Shields was a floor above us and nearly on the other side of the building spoke volumes of his abilities. The screams suggested he had other tricks up his sleeves, nastier tricks.

I love my whiskers; they are long and beautiful. They also sense air currents. Between them and my ears I knew that Sonja had moved over to the desk and the tech, and that Grady had pulled his side arm.

"You might want to hold off on that, unless you can see that is."

"Not a damn thing."

"The power's not out," the tech said. "I can still hear my computer, what's going on?"

Sonja's voice was cold. "A wannabe mage." With that she took something out from under her shirt, and suddenly the room was full of light. No, not her boobs. I mean, don't get me wrong, boobs are magical, but I doubt they can cut through this type of darkness. No, Sonja was holding up a pendant, the only one she wore, a Celtic Cross.

The computer screen was still aglow, the tech looked terrified out of his mind, and the ring of light only went a few yards before being swallowed up by the darkness.

"Claw." She threw me the necklace and I held it up high in my left hand, and drew one of my guns with my right.

Sonja grabbed both the flash drives and shoved them in the pocket of her blue jeans. She then put her right hand behind her back and firmly grasped nothing, and drew forth a glowing long sword.

For those that may only be familiar with swords from pop culture, the long sword in a lot of tabletop games is actually the arming sword. One handed, meant to be used with a shield, etc. This was a true long sword, one of her preferred weapons. It could be used in one hand or two. Its glow wasn't as fierce as that from her amulet, more muted, colder, but it went further than the light from the amulet.

The screams from upstairs had died down, I didn't know if that was a good sign or not.

"What's the plan?" Grady asked.

Sonja looked back at him. "If you want to go home to your family at the end of your shift, stay here, take care of him, lock the door, and pray. If you want to die so others don't have to, follow me, put the tech in one of those high security cages and follow me." With that she started moving out into the hall.

The tech didn't wait for whatever Grady was going to decide and got into one of the secure areas, clicking the door shut behind him. I, of course, was on Sonja's six. To my surprise Grady, mister 'I was about to be offered early retirement because I was just putting in hours', was right behind me.

As we made our way towards the stairs, the halls themselves twisted, pulsed, and seemed to breathe with evil intent. Strings of cancerous growth advanced further into our realm with every pulse. The color of the growths was a discord of colors that should not be, black, blue, red, pink, and a sheen of radioactive, glowing, iridescent green. The air became thick and hard to chew.

"What in God's name is going on?" Grady asked.

"We've been pushed sideways." I said.

"Sideways?"

Sonja spoke slowly. "The world is not the world. The world is layer after layer of reality. We're in the same place, but a different here."

"I'll bite?" Grady said.

"You really don't want to know." I said to him.

"What, it's not like it's hell… right? Right?"

I grinned at him, "Some would call it that."

"They'd be wrong. The Outer Void is much worse."

As we made our way further up, the further we went, the worse it got. Reality shuddered again, and as it did, the screams began anew. The first set of screams were human, the second were the denizens of this new nightmare. Sounds of steel slowly being torn like tissue, the grinding of nails on slate, the feeling of Styrofoam rubbing across teeth. Then the stairwell walls opened their eyes. Had the eyes been demonic, they would have been too much, but they were human, very human, and they were in pain, crying, and hopelessly lost.

Sonja opened the door that led into the open office, what I think they called a 'bull pit'. Her sword illuminated the room, but only barely. My mind wished it hadn't done the job as well as it did.

The cops, the police officers, the men and women who, for good or ill, made up the enforcement arm of the laws of the land, were all upright, but I wouldn't call it standing. Each and every one of them had a looseness to their stance that whispered that they weren't in control. No, that would be the black cancerous tendrils that were wrapped around them, inside them, filling holes like ears, nostrils, and screaming mouths plugged fast with the pulsating rubbery masses. Each twisted marionette had their side arm pulled, most of them were pointing their guns at us, waiting for the order to fire. Two of them held Blade fast, a third had their gun to her head. From the look on her face, I could tell she knew who was responsible for this travesty, and he had better kill her before she got free.

Said guilty party had the last of the cops, including the captain, acting as a human throne. A throne he didn't sit on, so much as lounge on.

"You know, when I first started learning magic, it was for tantric experimentation. It's only later that I realized it had more practical uses." He looked at the three of us. "You should all be puppets, happily bringing me what I require. I really wasn't expecting another mage."

"I'm no mage." Sonja said through clenched teeth.

The man nodded. "Interesting, I didn't know there were other disciplines that could counter magic."

I love Sonja. She and I have a similar sense of humor, something she proves time and time again. "Yeah well, if what you knew were plutonium, you wouldn't have enough to reach critical mass."

"Let me tell you how this is going to go. You are going to give me both drives, then go about your lives forgetting I ever existed. If you try anything stupid," half of the officers who had had their guns pointed at us, suddenly pointed their weapons at fellow officers. "I'll make sure that not only do you die, the girl dies, as does a good number of the fine men and women of law enforcement."

For a heartbeat, I didn't know what to do, I didn't know what Sonja would do. She's kind of big on the concept of not harming innocents, after all. I knew, knew she would do something. So, I waited for my chance, leveled my breathing and drew a bead on the would be mage. I caught Sonja flick her eyes over to me, and I knew it, whatever it was, was fixing to happen.

"1312." She said.

The man in the throne blinked, the cop behind us pointed his gun at Sonja. Both spoke at the same time.

"What?" Guess he didn't know what that meant.

Grady, of course, did. "Give him the fucking hard drives."

"I said." Sonja got a vicious look on her face. "All cops are bastards."

I watched as what she said, and its implications, played out on Mr. Shields' face. Sonja was willing to let most of the hostages die because she didn't consider them innocent. Shields had misjudged. He took and gave whatever mental command he had to give and all of the weapons started to move, away from the cops, away from us, and all pointed to Blade.

I didn't let it get that far. Mental commands are like anything else. You tell your brain what to do, the brain tells the body part, or in this case the puppets what to do. It takes time, concentration.

I made my gun bark at the asshole before he could realize his mistake. It was tempting to put him down permanently. But I didn't have that right. Not when I was trained within an inch of my life on how to disable a target needed for interrogation. Magic these days is all but unheard of. Mages exist, and this might seem like a hell of a spell, but trust me, it's not. It takes concentration, a lot of it.

Double tap straight to the kneecaps. I honestly wouldn't have tried it had he been sitting on his thrown. But no, he was lounging. As such both of his knees were wide open with only a wall on the other side.

He went down.

All of the police dropped to the ground, puppets with their strings cut.

Two unseen 'things' peeled loose from the artificial shadows created by this ass and launched themselves at Sonja. These things were twisted, smoldering, fire embers given the shape of massive dogs. Well, dog-like anyway. Dogs don't have six legs with fangs that drip something red.

Sonja dropped her sword and did something I rarely get to see her do. She flicked out her right arm, and a red-hot glowing chain sprang forth from out of her arm. She used it like a whip and caught one of the dogs across the face, forcing it to hit the ground, hard.

The other had been going for me, me and my pretty face. Me who was still dealing with the fact that I, too, had been telling my body to do something else just a heartbeat ago. I turned my gun towards the bad dog. Said dog suddenly mid-flight decided it was going to go off to the left and turn its head back to its shoulder.

It took a moment for me to register what happened.

Grady had shot the damn thing.

That's right, he had had his gun out too, and was pointing it at Sonja.

He didn't shoot Sonja.

He shot the dog.

I so owed him a beer.

Blade meanwhile had gone over to young wannabe master Derik who was holding his leg and whimpering, and kicked him in his face. As her boot struck home, his lights went out, and with that, the lights came back on. With the mage not only distracted, but unconscious, reality violently reasserted itself. With that, the two whatever they were, stayed in the dark world we had been in.

The captain, who still had a bleeding suspect sitting on her and the other officers who had made up his chair... and apparently his lawyer too, pushed the bastard off and did the only sensible thing to do.

"What in the hell just happened?"

Sonja looked at her. "Count your blessings that you don't have memory of it."

Chapter 30

The slamming of the door rattled the glass. "What the hell was that ACAB bullshit?" Given that it was Grady asking, and not the Captain whose office we were in, made her look at him as if he lost his damn mind.

Sonja raised an eyebrow. "Do you want the truth, or something to be mad at?"

Grady crossed his arms, and seemed to be thinking it over.

The captain meanwhile pursed her lips. "So, we have a mage, with a missing kneecap and a concussion on his way to the hospital. I, and every other cop here, have a raging headache. And none of the cameras in this place caught anything but static."

Sonja kept staring at Grady, and Grady kept staring at her.

Oh well. "Well, you see, mage boy shoved us somewhere not nice and turned off the lights. Sonja gave me a light ball to play with and drew one of her swords, and when we got up here all of you were being used as marionettes by the jerk wad who was threating to shoot all of us and half of you."

Blade who had been allowed to follow us this time added, "Claw shot him freeing you, and I knocked him out sending us back to reality."

The captain looked us over, then asked Grady, "Is that true?"

He broke his staring contest with Sonja. "Yeah." As he spoke, he seemed to deflate. "That's what happened."

She nodded, then looked at Sonja. "And what does all cops are bastards have to do with this? And I want the truth, not something to be mad about."

"He was basically shunting us over, and using the planes 'attributes' against us. Think of it like hypnosis. Those things can control a person, but they can't make them do something that is against their morals." She gave a shrug. "When he realized I didn't care if a few cops got shot, he told them to point at the victim. While some of the cops might kill each other, a lot fewer would shoot a white woman, fewer still a white woman who was smaller than they were." She shrugged. "I needed the guns off those cops."

I watched as the wheels began turning in the two humans' head. I could actually hear the moment Grady's hamster died. The captain just nodded. "So, what exactly did he want?"

Sonja put both drives up on her desk. "The encryption key for the crypto that the cartel uses."

Both officers looked at the flash drives as if they were live grenades.

In a way, they were. The blockchain is nothing more than a ledger that is copied to the computers of all the users of that system. As a self-correcting system it meant that if someone tried to give themselves a few zeros those zeros wouldn't match anyone else's ledger. Originally it was billed as unbreakable, untraceable, uncontrollable currency. The FBI of course had already proved they could indeed track it when part of that money was stolen by a user. The things on the desk could either bring the whole thing down or allow the government to infiltrate the whole network on a scale that made what the FBI managed to pull off seem like small potatoes.

"Definitely a motive for murder." Whispered the captain.

Blade hugged herself. "Fucking wanker. I shudda done more than use his head for a football."

Sonja was frowning. "Only, the cartel didn't know that Rayzor was dead, and Derik had one of the spell bombs set up in his place." Letting out a breath, she shook her head.

Grady put a hand on her shoulder. "You're over thinking it. The Cartel didn't know she was dead, that's why the spell was in her place and in his."

Two mages. The key to a lot of money. The DA would have enough evidence to put ol' Derik away for the rest of his life.

Blade was the one who dropped the bomb. "They aren't going to stop looking for this." She was right, the Cartel wouldn't stop, not until they had this key back. Back, or knew it was destroyed.

Like I said, live grenades.

"Who knows we have these?" The captain asked.

Grady answered. "Just the people in this room and Tom down in evidence."

I could not only hear my heartbeat, but the heartbeat of every person in the room. They weren't grenades, they were time bombs.

"Shit." She got up from behind her desk and went to the door. She opened it and said to the men and women who were there, all of whom were nursing a massive headache. "Someone go downstairs and get me Tom. Tell him not to say a damn thing and get him now. If he does say something, tell him I will make sure he is not only fired but that charges will be pressed. Tell him he better not have said a god damn thing to anyone else either."

Panicked people do stupid shit. I raised my hand to tell her what she had just done, but she held up a hand and stopped me. "Not a word. All of you consider yourself detained for the moment and take a seat." With that she picked up her office phone and dialed a number. "Get me the DA, not the ADA, the god damn DA and the head of the fucking FBI. Get them here now and tell them it's Savage shit."

Savage shit.

She just invoked Kyle.

Fuck, she was right, this was definitely Savage shit, even if he wasn't actually involved.

Tom came in, looking like a man who remembered what he saw. Given he wasn't being used as a puppet, he probably did.

"I haven't said anything to anyone." Were the first words out of his mouth.

The Captain nodded. "Good." She waved a dismissive hand at the officers who had brought him up. Heading back to the door, she looked out at the assembled officers. "Everyone, we just had a major mage incursion. No one is going anywhere until we get cleared. God only knows what condition we're really in." She nodded to herself. "Someone get on the line to the Black Squad and get them to come in and start clearing people." With that she closed the door and went back and sat down. "That will keep them from talking." She let out a sigh. "I knew it as soon as it was out of my mouth. But now they will be busy following protocol. They will think I called for Tom because of what the guy did…" With that she sat back down in her office chair.

It was a pretty good save. Had she left it at the fuck up, someone might have put two and two together and leaked info to the cartel. Now they were too busy worrying that their balls were going to drop off from magical radiation.

Yeah, we had some time.

I hoped we had enough.

Chapter 31

Oh SH*T

While the Black Squad and their people were out there dealing with the aftermath of a mage attack, the head of the local FBI and the DA had joined us in the office. The captain proceeded to explain things quickly and succinctly, meeting all the highlights and not leaving anything important out. The result was now everyone was staring at the time bomb in the room.

Mr. Suit spoke first. "Do they know we have it?"

"Unknown." The captain said. "At this point the evidence points to two mages not of the cartel, both low powered according to Claw and Sonja. We have the one in custody."

The DA spoke. "I can't even look at that thing without a warrant, and I certainly don't have probable cause. That crypto is registered and the company that owns it appears to be legitimate." FBI raised an eyebrow. The DA shrugged, "A lot of unsavory people use it, we've looked into it before."

"If the company is legit, then we have their stolen property." The captain said. "We contact them and ask if they wish to press charges. Simple as that."

She was, of course, correct.

No one moved.

"That doesn't guarantee the cartel will stop looking for it. After all," he looked at the DA, "I'm betting you haven't been able to tie the company to them." The DA pursed his lips and shook his head. "I thought not."

"We could do a press conference." Tom said. All three of the upper brass looked at him with stares that could strip paint off walls. "Or not."

The DA nodded. "It's not a completely bad idea, but if we do so, it's going to cause the currency to lose value. The company could and would sue the hell out of the city for that, and all of us would be lucky to land a job picking up trash in the tunnel."

They continued to stare at the drives.

Blade slowly raised her hand. All three of them slowly turned their heads until they were facing her.

"Why don't ya just, you know, use it?"

The DA shook his head, the captain looked horrified, but the FBI guy spoke. "Trust me, I would love to do nothing more than to do just that. But if we did, nothing we learned could ever be acted on. It would be 'tainted fruit'."

"Fruit of the poisonous tree." The DA corrected. "No judge worth a damn would ever allow it. Hell, if defense could even suggest that we had this and looked at it, about ten of the cases my office is working on would go up in smoke."

"I gots an idea." Everyone turned to look at me. "I was worried about a leak, cuz, you know. But let's say there is a leak. We make them work for us."

The three of them exchanged glances. "How?" That one word was asked with great suspicion.

"Simple. We take and call the company; tell them we stumbled across a drive with one of their security keys on it and would like to return it. Then we tell or I should say, let it be known we have something from the company and are returning it. The only people who know what that is, is us, the cartel, and the guy who stole it. So, the house gossip does our work for us and lets a mole or plant or whatever you call them say what we want them to, but the cartel knows what it is. No one gets sued or shot." I was rather proud of that idea.

The humans... not so much. I watched as they mulled it over, saw their hamsters run in starts and stops. Each of them shared a look I had seen way to much of in my short life, 'she's nuts'. Slowly, however, their brains' little wheels caught traction.

"That's not that bad an idea. I mean, not exactly what she said, but yes. It could work." Mr. DA said. Then he looked over at the three of us. "I'm sorry, what exactly was your role in this?"

"Well, we were hired to look into the death of a trans woman. The rest just, well, kind of happened as we were investigating." I flicked an ear. We were fixing to get the brush off, I could feel it.

Sonja spoke up. "The mother of the victim wanted us to look into it, to rebuild her child's last days. The gentleman who Detective Grady gave you who was so willing to turn on his cartel friends had been told by the mage that we just took down who she was and the two of them blackmailed her into being a mule. After she got back, she hid both hard drives, flash drives she had doubtlessly stolen from her black mailers probably for leverage. She hid one in her apartment, and one at her gym. After that, someone…" Sonja's face fell. "Someone shot her, in the back." She cocked her head. "But neither of them, none of them would have done that. One needed the drugs from her and didn't know she was dead… the other, he didn't know she was dead either, or else he wouldn't have booby trapped her apartment."

I knew it was coming. I had seen this time and time again. The confusion first, then the revelation.

"We need to get to the Smith's." She said as she stood up. "They're in danger." She rattled off their address then whistled. I would have paid good money to have had a camera when a Gothed out grey hearse was suddenly in the middle of the Captain's office. All 4 front doors of the vehicle opened, Sonja slide into the driver seat, Blade and I jumped in too. "Grady, you coming?" She cried out the other opened door.

This was it for Grady, the moment of truth. Did he stay, accept retirement, go home and lead a good life? Or did he throw all of that away?

I grinned as he jumped in.

All four doors shut as one, as the two in the back put on seat belts.

"Do I want to know how you got a car into that office?"

I looked back at him and cackled. "This is Mortis, he's the transportation."

With that we were off driving though the twilight world that both the transportation and the transportee called home. As we slid through the darkness at an alarming rate of speed, I slowly started to put together what Sonja did. She was apparently operating under the idea that Rayzor's death hadn't been connected to either of the leads we'd been chasing. Didn't that make me all warm and gooey inside.

Oh kay... start from the top.

One, she had been shot in the back. A detail so minor I hadn't much thought of it. That meant that at bare minimum she had her back to the person. Walking away? Maybe running away. Then she had been beaten.

Two she wasn't killed for the drugs or the flash drives. She wasn't robbed. She had to have been killed for a reason, but three of the motives were now smoke on the wind.

Wait, where had they found her? Oh yeah. The next street over... from the Synagogue fire. A definite hate crime.

My mind clicked the same as hers did. The little bastard was the only one not to mistake Blade for Rayzor. "Son of a bitch."

Sonja nodded. "Yep."

We slid into the real world again, and as we did, we came across chaos. The Smith family home was on fire.

Bad news, the house was burning, and it was burning fast enough I didn't need to test the air to know someone had used an accelerant. As I got out into the air, which one it was hit my nose: turpentine. Good news, mom was on the front lawn screaming at her son as her husband lay on the ground. Bad news, he didn't look conscious, and the delinquent was holding a pipe wrench.

Grady and Blade were out just after me, with Sonja getting out last. I made a bee line for mom and dad; Grady pulled his weapon and pointed it at the kid. "It's over, drop the wrench."

Before he could act, before he could turn, something threw him back, back towards the burning house. In the dancing light of the flames, I could see a shimmer. Rayzor had found her killer. All hell was about to break loose.

Chapter 32

I had never seen the birth of a wraith before, that was what I was witnessing now. To begin with, Rayzor was a shimmer among shimmers of heat from the fire. As she 'slapped' her killer around more, she became deeper, darker, more shadowy, and a lot more real. So did her screams. The cry of a wraith can kill all on its own. The cries of this newborn one, this being born one? Either way, they were painful.

I had got over to the mom and dad and realized dad was out cold with a bonk to the head, but he was breathing. I did not envy the poor bastard the headache he was going to have if he survived. Speaking of which, I needed to do what I could to make sure that happened.

Blade was trying to comfort her new aunt as she watched her cousins fight. Grady, Grady didn't know what to do. It's not like a bullet can stop a ghost. He made his way over and started helping me.

Sonja? Sonja was calm, dead calm, as she walked up and spoke to Rayzor.

"I know what he did, so do the cops." Despite the cacophony of the fire, and the sounds of reality itself ripping and reknitting with each of the birthing wraiths strikes, I had no problem whatsoever hearing and understanding her. "Rayzor, if you kill him, you can't come back from that."

Yeah, sorry honey, I don't think she cares, ran through my mind as the ghost tried once more to push her own little brother back into the flames of their family home.

Slowly, still speaking calmly, she got between them. "Please Rayzor. Please don't do this."

With the distraction, Edward made it to his feet. "You want me you fag, well here I am!"

A tendril of shadows grew from Rayzor's right arm as she swung it once more at her brother, trying to knock him back into the fire of his own making. Sonja caught it with her left hand. As soon as she did, the shadowy part of it dissolved, leaving only her bloody arm.

Still Edward raged. "You think you're so fucking special. You're a fucking traitor is what you are."

"Don't worry about him. He's going to jail, and he's going to be gone a long time."

Rayzor lunged at him again, trying to get around to her brother. As she did, Sonja caught her. "It's not your fault. None of it was your fault. Not the drugs, not the rape, none of it." She hugged the now very solid Rayzor with all her might. As they went from that painful ever-increasing wail to the sounds of a woman sobbing.

"You're not wrong, you're not bad. You didn't do this; you didn't deserve this." She said as she rocked the woman. As Sonja's words sank in, the grief started pouring out of the spirit. "You're not wrong, you're not bad. Don't let him steal from you any more than he already has. You are not wrong, not bad, this isn't your fault."

At that, Edward finally lost it. "Not his fault? It's always been his fault. They gave the faggot everything he wanted, ignoring me. They hated me. When he fucking ran away like the coward he is, they turned on me. Nothing I did was ever good enough. Then I found out dad had been going to see the fag. Probably to get his dick sucked…"

With those words, the woman in Sonja's arms flared into a black flame. That flame fully engulfed both herself and Sonja. Edward scrambled from the heat of it. Out of that flame, a red and black flaming chain whip lashed out, and hit the bastard right in his damn mouth.

I admit it, I cheered.

From inside the flames, I heard these words.

I AM, WE ARE, HE IS NOT.

As quickly as they flared, they were gone. There, in Sonjas grip, still being hugged, was a ghostly version of Rayzor. She was decked out in full goth, emo, punk attire. Finally, Sonja let go.

"Go on. Go to your family, say your goodbyes. God knows you've earned it." With that, Rayzor, looking a hell of a lot better than she did moments before, was suddenly right beside us.

"**Mom, don't worry. Dad is going to be ok.**" With that she bent down and stroked her dad's forehead.

Across the way, Edward had gotten back to his feet. Where the whip had struck his face, a bruise was forming rapidly. He made his way over to the dropped wrench and picked it up, hatred was burning in his eyes.

"I'll get back to you in a moment. I got to take care of the freak first." As he spoke, his words were... different. They were off. Too much growl, too much grind. He turned and brandished the wrench, and as he did, it caught fire. "I quite agree. We kill the bitch first, then the cat. Then you can have the faggot while I take care of mother and father." He started walking towards Sonja, as he did, I watched as he... how do I put this? As he followed himself, half a step behind.

Grady finally with something to do, something to understand, went full cop. "You, drop the wrench, put your hands above your head, and spread your feet apart."

Edward didn't stop.

"I am warning you, drop your weapon and put your hands up."

Edward didn't stop.

In fact, he had made it to Sonja, who, for some reason, was just standing there swaying. He slowly raised his arm and went to strike.

At that point both I and Grady had the same idea. We both shot the bastard. Grady was much more... reserved let's say. He only shot twice. I meanwhile was freaked out by the fact that the son of a bitch had a shadow him that was half a heartbeat behind, I emptied my clip. Eight .45 ACP, air mailed right into center of mass.

Edward staggered back from the hits.

But he didn't fall.

Oh no, instead he turned and looked at me and Grady, as he did his eyes flashed red.

Well fuck.

Sonja seemed to snap out of it at that point. She shook her head and realized that something was going on. I think it was because of all the gunfire. She took a look back, saw the ruined hole in Edward's chest, a hole of raw meat that was reknitting itself while we watched, and seemed to realize a maniac was at her back and she was unarmed.

She made a mad dash to the car.

Grady fired again, that knocked the bastard back again. "Why isn't she whipping out that chain thing or one of her light swords?"

"Spirit swords? Against steel?" I pointed at the wrench.

"What? It counters her magic?"

Actually, that wasn't as dumb a question as it sounded. "No, her blades aren't real, that is. You've seen how reality deals with not real things."

He got it, and as he did, he emptied the last of his ammo into the guy. "So, what do we do, cuz I don't know if you've noticed or not, but shooting him isn't doing shit."

Yeah, I had noticed. "Well, it slows him down." I took out my second .45 and slowed him down again. "Maybe if we get lucky, he'll fall over." Yeah, I sounded like I believe that with the same conviction that I believe in a flat earth. Sure, it could happen, but I'd be damned if I had ever seen any evidence or even a good argument for it.

"So, what now?"

Abigail got in front of us. "Edward Jeffery Smith, you stop this right now."

Wow, she broke out the full name on him. For a heartbeat I even dared to believe it would work.

Then dollar store Jayson Vorhies started marching our way, and me without any more ammo to give him as a welcoming present.

"Fuck this." I reached behind my back and pulled my Ka-Bar. "Let's dance, ugly."

Thankfully he came right at me with that.

Unfortunately, he came right at me with that.

Yay me.

Duck first, dodge second, cut third. Dude had zero hand to hand training. Dodge lunge, dodge fist, dodge wrench, cut two. Unfortunately, the cuts were having the same effect as the bullets.

"Holy fuck, is that a sword?"

It was stupid, I knew it was stupid, I looked back anyway.

Yes, I paid for it. I got hit square in the chest with the wrench.

Yes, it was a sword. A long sword to be exact, a real one.

No, Sonja wasn't doing a slow cinematic walk, but God, wouldn't that look bad ass. No, she wasn't jumping through the air with a mad downward power swing. Again, that too would have been bad ass.

Instead? She was riding in on her pale horse, long sword at the ready.

Edward didn't bother to try to fight that, he ran.

I wish that was the end of it. I really do. I mean it should have been, right?

I could hear the sirens of the local emergency responders. Dumb ass had broken and ran. Rayzor wasn't going to turn into a wraith. And Sonja was a red head on horseback with a big honking sword. That should have been the end and me and my bruised, possibly broken, ribs could get some medical help.

"No, no I won't. Yes. Sure. I accept."

Fucking Edward…

The wrench turned into a great big honking sword of its own, and the way the boy was standing changed. Edward the Doofus didn't know how to fight. Edward the Barbarian was apparently a different matter.

Chapter 33

The wrench was a fairly standard, if slightly rusted, pipe wrench red. The swords cross guard, pommel, and the middle line kept that vibrant red. The handle meanwhile looked like a twisted iron bar. It was going to turn that poor boy's hand into so much hamburger... Not that the thing that was in control now cared about such things.

"Well, well, well, you must be the new mantle bearer." Sir Edward growled out. "I must say, you are most certainly not an improvement. I was friends with the last one. Now, he knew how to keep his nose out of things that did not concern him. It's a shame that you killed him. I simply must return the favor."

Sonja slid off of Mortis' back with an almost languid grace. She rolled her neck as she lazily stalked towards whatever Edward was now.

"I didn't kill him, I just replaced him."

Edward snarled. "Impossible!" He pointed the tip of his blade at her face. "If that were true you would be..." He trailed off. "No matter, you're still mortal." His sword became writhed in flames. "What is it you human's say? Have at thee?"

"Not even close." She stepped forward and began her attack.

High strike from the left, into waterfall, high strike to the right, same result. Then he did his own strikes with her matching him block for block. In the technical it seems they were an even match. This wasn't a match, and technique wouldn't decide this battle.

Each and every time the being struck a blow against Sonja, his blade would spark and flare, sending embers or bits of hot metal flying at her. Most were no longer glowing red by the time they hit her skin… most.

"I see the fear in your eyes, mantel bearer, your resolve will not hold. I think this boy would be well suited to the job you're about to vacate with your life." He started hammering her with quicker and quicker strikes. "Especially given why he killed his sister."

Sonja flinched back once more. "Oh please. You're not scaring me enough to take you seriously yet. I don't…" she dodged a blow from his fist meant for her head. "Don't believe you have enough rank to do so. I've just got to wait till you've exhausted the vessel. At that point," She gave a grunt as she threw him off of herself, "I'll just exorcise you."

At that he started laughing. "I'm using far less of my power than you think, girl. The boy has a latent healing ability. I've only had to activate it to heal the wounds you and yours have inflicted."

Grady had long given up trying to shoot the kid, and had helped me get dad as comfortable as a concussion would let him be. He looked at me, then at what was going on.

"What the fuck is happing here?"

"What it is, ain't exactly clear." He looked at me like I had lost my mind. There's no accounting for taste. "The boy has made a pact with the demon, and now the two of them are playing highlander."

"She has to cut off his head?"

With the kid having a healing ability... "I hope not." Sonja had a thing about innocents. Though, I'm not sure this guy counted as one to her. "But chuckles just took away one of her options."

"Why is the boy bulking up?"

"His name is Edward, and he's the one who killed Rayzor."

"I got that, but why kill his sister?"

I blinked at the guy, "Nazi, trans sister, synagogue... come on man. Keep up."

"So, what do we do?"

It was Blade that answered him. "Only thing we can do mate, get the civies out of here." She pointed at the ambulance, the fire truck, and the cops who were pulling up. "Because if that thing is what I think it is, if things start going bad, it will start aiming for them." I looked at her funny. "What? So? I'm a witch."

Mrs. Smith actually took that better than I thought as we got Mr. Smith over to the ambulances.

The sounds of steel on steel didn't stop as we did so, and by the time I turned back, the asshole had driven her to her knees. That's when he made his mistake, he kicked her in her face. I watched the blood spray out. Some people have glass jaws, she had something similar. Her nose was just this side of being an anime blood fountain.

His kick was nothing to sneeze at, it knocked her to the ground. That's when he made his second mistake. He stopped to gloat.

"How pathetic. You? Have the Mantle of something so much greater than yourself. How?" He spit on her. "A worthless girl, you don't deserve what you have been given, and you already admitted that you didn't earn it. Let me relieve you of that burden." With that he swung his sword down in an arch that would divorce her head and her neck.

She rolled.

I knew what was coming next, I had seen it before.

Sonja, well, she calls herself a Celt, a Celt and a mystic who follows the teachings of the carpenter from the Middle East. I can't say yes or no to that. Lord knows she doesn't act like one, at least not one I'd ever seen.

At times like this?

I believe her.

She stood, and as she did three sets of shadow wings unfurled around her, the sword in her hand began to glow. Both of those can be unsettling to see. But, hey, we live in a world with powered people, people who can chuck a car at you, people born with real wings they can fly with. Hell, I know a girl that can read anything you put in front of her as if it were English. So no, glowing swords and shadow 'wings' didn't mean much.

It was the eyes. No, they weren't white or black, or even red or purple. She actually wishes they would go purple; she likes purple. No, they were green. Not like with the others where her whole eye turns, oh no. That might look bad ass. No this was just her normal, usually steel grey irises, only now, they were the same green that Disney uses as a shorthand for a villain. What was far worse was that look. If you been in the shit, either as a soldier, or a poor bastard caught in a warzone, or any one of a dozen other cruelties humans do to each other, you know this look. No one's home, she's somewhere else, and you are going to die. A soulless thousand-yard stare that means one thing and one thing only, death has come for you.

Yeah, it wasn't lost on the dude. He went to run.

That hellfire whip of hers slithered out of her arm and she lashed out with it, wrapping it around his feet. Jerking she tied them together and snatched.

He went down, and she began to reel her catch in. As the thing in the boy got closer, it began to scream. Sounds like that aren't meant to come out of human throats. When she got him close enough, she reached down and into his chest, the thing's cries stopped mid-sound. She then literally pulled the thing out of Edward.

What came out of Edward was something that looked like a human covered in tar or made of tar. I asked Sonja about it later and she told me we see what we expect to see, and I had watched too much Star Trek. Grady was the old cartoon mascot guy. The one in the red suit with the pitchfork. She assured him that the thing hadn't been the devil.

Either way, as soon as it was free of the boy it started to ooze and bubble and steam as it literally evaporated away. The last thing it said was, "Banish me."

Sonja just said, "No."

It should have been over then and there, probably would have been, if it weren't for Edward.

The little fucker had a gun. Why he hadn't used it earlier was beyond me, but he didn't. Apparently now was his big chance, he took it out and shot Sonja, dead center of the chest.

She dropped the thing. It started crawling over to the boy, and damn him, he started crawling over to it. I was too stunned to know what to do.

Grady took care of that. "Drop the gun and get on the ground." Edward kept crawling towards the thing. "I said drop your weapon and put your hands on your head." He actually hadn't, but I wasn't about to argue. "This is your final warning." Still Edward crawled towards the thing, and the thing made a feeble attempt to get to him.

Grady discharged his firearm, straight into the head of the whatever the fuck it was. With that the last of the oily son of a bitch lost coherency and it literally fell to glop as it hit the ground. Edward let out a low moan, then a curse, then he rolled over and went to point the gun at us. Grady had taken that time to get close, so he kicked the damn gun out of the little bastard's hand.

Mister man wasn't much interested in fighting anymore after that. No, he just rocked, screamed, and sobbed.

I made a mad four-legged dash over to Sonja.

She was, much to my delight, still breathing. I ripped her top opened and prayed that she wore a bra. She did. The blood… well she wasn't bleeding. I'd seen this before too, she was in shock, she wouldn't bleed until she wasn't. I did a quick check. Wound on the front, none on the back. The damn thing was still inside.

Fuck.

I put the ruins of her shirt over the wound and pressed down.

Sonja started coughing. "Need, need to breath cat." She said in a weak voice.

"You need to not bleed to death you dumb shit."

'It's not that deep." She lifted her head slightly and looked at her chest. "I liked that shirt."

"Damn the shirt."

"Claw?"

I looked her in the eyes. "What?"

"I went shadow."

I blinked at her. Shadow? What the hell did shadow have to do with... I pulled the shirt off her chest and looked. She was bleeding now, but the sternum wasn't shattered. The bullet should have shattered...

I sat down and started hyperventilating. When she started laughing, I started beating her about the head and shoulders.

"I thought you were dead you dumb shit!"

To her credit, she just kept laughing.

Chapter 34

Hospitals, what is there to say? We had been in and out of them for various reasons; talk to a suspect, see to a psych call, talk to a suspect... Now I was watching Sonja get patched up. She freaked when the doctor came at her with a needle. She's deathly afraid of the things. Guns? No big. Swords and knives? You better get ready to eat them if you point one at her. Needles? She literally started crying as the doc came out to numb the area. By the time he was done stitching her up she was watching the doctor's technique.

Guess sewing needles don't count.

Blade was in with Mr. and Mrs. Smith waiting to hear how bad Mr. Smith's condition was. When I checked in on them, he still wasn't awake, but the doctors weren't too worried. Blade was being a lot of help and support for Abigail, asking the woman all the questions about her new family. She was surprised she had another aunt and a couple of cousins.

Sonja, Grady, and I were unwinding, while we waited for her to be discharged. She was shot after all. We alternated between bull shitting, and Grady was asking questions to make sure he understood everything. That was when five foot two inches,

154 lbs. of blonde trouble walked in. There was a knock at the door, and as usual Sonja said "Yes?" rather than come in. I think it's from her time dealing with the fae.

Amanda Strongheart poked her head in. "Alright if I intrude?" Amanda was both a friend and a cop. In fact in some ways she was THE cop when it came to dealing with the bullshit we'd been dealing with for the last couple of days. She was the head of the Black Squad.

Black Squad, in brief, handled the relatively few supernatural crimes in the city. The shit that went bump in the night did exist, but if you took all the crime that element committed, known and unknown, and added all it together it wouldn't equal what happened in a small town in a year. There just weren't that many supernatural shenanigans.

Which was why her not being here until now had my interest.

"Here chick! Come for a bite?" She rolled her eyes at the old inside joke.

"Came to see if you two were all right, first and foremost." She stepped in and looked at Sonja. "Getting shot doesn't look good on you hun."

Sonja gave a one arm shrug, still pulled her stitches. You could tell from the way her eyes crinkled. "Yeah well, I'd ask why you weren't here earlier, but you needed to see if Grady was worth it."

Grady looked dumb founded. "What?"

"Well, is he?"

Sonja nodded. "He cares. It's why he was burned out. Give him something real to do and you're golden."

He looked back and forth between the two of them, then his gaze fell back on Sonja. "You knew?"

She gave him a weak smile. "She didn't interfere with a case that was, by mandate, in her jurisdiction. The only way that would happen is if she were aware of the case and decided it didn't need her input. Once your captain said this was a test?" She shrugged. "It wasn't hard to figure out."

Amanda let out a laugh. "I still think you two should come and work for me. God Sonja, I could really use that brain of yours sometimes."

Before now, that offer had always been flatly rejected. "See to Grady first."

"Fair enough. So, what about it, detective? Want to trade in your gold shield for a black one?"

He thought about it for a moment. "Shit going to get as weird as it did with these two?"

Amanda gave him her straight face. "This? Oh no, this was simple shit. Everything involved was human, for the most part. The one thing that wasn't was, well not to put too fine a point on it, evil. You managed not to blow the kid away, brought him in and he's turning on his buddies as we speak. You did good. But that was soft ball. What I am offering you is both hard ball and a chance at the majors."

"Does it come with more pay?"

"Nope. But at the end of the night, you get to know you did make a difference."

He nodded, "I'm in."

Amanda smiled at him. "Good. I won't disappoint you, so don't disappoint me." Then she looked back at us. "Well?"

"Well, I guess we could pull a Holmes for you. Consulting detective kind of thing."

She grinned. "Excellent." She then poked her head outside. "Hey, Mike. Get this man a desk and get him started on his paperwork for this case. Show him how I like things and give him the dime tour of home."

From outside the room, a voice, presumably Mike, said "Will do. Come on rook, let's get you up to speed."

Grady walked about with a look of mock annoyance on his face. "Who you calling a rook? I got tee shirts older than you." The door closed and left us alone with Amanda.

She turned back to Sonja; the smile had evaporated like dew at sunrise. "Ok, so what the fuck happened?"

Sonja readjusted herself. "Demon, small potatoes. Couldn't have been more than a minor. Not a feeder mind you, this was the real deal."

"How the hell did that happen? I thought you had to invite those fucking things in."

I winced, "The kid did. Hell, he'd been having a fucking running one sided conversation with the damn thing."

"Is that the reason for the change in attitude? Something big is coming?"

But to my surprise Sonja shook her head no. "No, actually. Jess has most of that well in hand... no." She let out a sigh. "This, case. I realized I could actually do some good. I trust you like I trust Kyle. And if your vetting of Grady is normal for how you pick your people, I think I might actually do some good helping you."

She relaxed at the 'no the world isn't ending' part of things. "So, why not join up completely then. It would definitely solve some of your money problems." Her face softened, "We both know you hate asking Kyle for money."

She nodded. "Yeah, that's true. Though I think I might need to get the hell over that. But no. I still have other things I have to do; things you know you don't want to be involved with." She let out another sigh. "I love you girl, but the less reason people have to suspect you? The better off we're all going to be."

But the cop shook her head. "Nobody figured it out last time. And besides, I've had to sit for stitches and get operated on."

"Yes, but you are immortal. You, your husband, your whole damn society. I'm too much of a risk for you to actually be under you. All that has to happen is you covering for one of my trips, and then they start nesting up your ass the way they nest up Kyle's. I won't do that to you. A good cop is always on call. I can't be, and you can't cover for me."

"Fine, consulting detective it is. I'm sure I can come up with some reason to have you sort of on staff... there must be something."

I held up a hand, "A consultant for the department. The rest of the houses hire them all the time. Given what you work in, I doubt they will mind you hiring us."

She nodded. "I'll check. Thanks kitty cat."

I nodded at her. "Oh, you going to be at Sunday dinner?"

At that her face lit up. "Sorry, its mine and Harper's Anniversary, and he's actually in town. I'll see if we can swing by, but he says he's got something planned."

With that we shot the shit for a little longer, and I wondered what the old man had planned for his wife. Oh well, something told me I would find out Sunday.

Epilogue

Back Home

I helped the slightly wounded barbarian berserker back into her home, when we got a hell of a surprise. Two of them actually. The first one had tidied up the place. It was the Sidhe that had confessed her love for Sonja, the woman named Betha.

Sonja blinked at her. "I've missed something."

"Hardly your fault." Betha said. "You slept when I made my confession. Master Donovan had accidentally enticed you in his concern. We needed you woken, and I provided the kiss."

Sonja, it seemed, took it in stride. "I see." Then she shifted uncomfortably as the words sank in. "Oh, I see."

"I am not dismissed if that is your worry. You have done me no harm." She took a deep breath. "Master Donovan has offered me a boon. I asked for a chance to ask and follow through. If you will have me that is."

Sonja turned bright red. "I see. Um…"

Betha smiled. "I am Sabetha, your servant and caretaker if you will have me. I will be honored to be your maid and see to your needs." Then her face softened, and I watched her switch away from her normal mode of speech. "Come now," she looked around, "I think you could use the help, and... I," But she couldn't bring herself to say it.

Sonja stepped up and petted the woman's face. "You are not betraying him." Betha nodded. "I know, it hurts, but Betha," She took Betha's face in her hands. "I have had you in my heart since the first night. I adore Donovan... he is the only man I will let touch me. I find my feelings of attraction are more, feminine." With those words she kissed her.

As she backed off, Betha curtsied low. Like wow low.

Sonja chuckled. "As for us? We'll have to find out what us is and what works. But, I am afraid I am far less formal that our dear Donovan."

"I shall endeavor to become more used to your, style."

She nodded, "Good."

That was when the front door burst opened.

The three of us turned, defensive stance and hell ready to rain down on whomever was this stupid.

The door bounced, rebounded, and opened again to show Blade.

"Bloody hell, will someone give me a hand?" She had bags tossed over her shoulder, another two under her arm, and one in each hand. Banging the door opened would have been the only way to get the thing opened with all she was carrying. "And there's more in the cab. Bloody hell."

Sonja went and grabbed the right side, Betha the left. Both of them were hospitality oriented.

I was a cat. I'm curiosity oriented. "What are you doing?"

"Moving in?" The way she said it was both a duh this is obvious, and a please, please, please kind of thing. "I asked Sonja."

Sonja shrugged. "She wanted a fresh start."

"Besides, that Donovan guy said I was an old line. I kind of want to find out what that means."

Betha laughed at that. "A woman with a quest. I like it."

"Yeah, and well, I saw what those two consider paperwork and well, I'm going to be their secretary."

What did you know? We were two, now we were four. "Welcome aboard."

About the Author

R. F. DeAngelis is Trans Woman and activist with a chronic pain condition and dyslexia. She honestly believes that the story will set us free and refuses to give up despite the curve balls life throws at all of us. She has been in a committed relationship for 20 years and is a practice of BDSM as a top with a wonderful family and support structure she loves very much.

What do I say about myself? Well, I am... Me? The things about me people might find most interesting are these five things. I have been in the BDSM lifestyle since 99 and a top since 01. I am a trans woman. I'm dyslexic. I have DID. Oh, and I play D&D.
While my life isn't sunshine and roses, I prefer the night and the thorns anyway. I persevere. I don't care how hard something is, I will do my best to ride it out until I master it.

My love for writing comes from the fact that books saved my life as a teen and young adult. So, I'm paying it forward.

We're On the Web

Come find us for updates, merch, and more at MDiro.com

You can join our community. get updates, and more.

Catch me on Twiter at @RFDeAngelis

or on FaceBook at M'Diro United

On TikTok as Five Authors in a Meatsuit

For a full list or work go to MDiro.com/books

Printed in the USA
CPSIA information can be obtained
at www.ICGtesting.com
CBHW031637230724
12052CB00004B/21